"Why are you crying.

Michael asked. "Are you hurt?"

Yes! her mind screamed. But it wasn't her knee. She didn't know what it was. She couldn't think when he looked at her with such compassion.

"Dana, talk to me."

A ragged breath shook her body. Damn him and his dogged determination to get inside her head! She opened her eyes, angry with him for making her tell him, for making her confront herself. "Can't you see?" she cried. "I hate being helpless and dependent! I hate being a burden!"

"It's normal for you to feel those things," Michael said softly. "But they're not true."

Her emerald-green eyes gazed up at him, and he wondered if it were possible for a man to drown on dry land just by looking at her. Her wide, full lips were parted slightly, and with a jolt Michael realized he wanted to kiss her. Badly.

Dear Reader,

Welcome to Silhouette **Special Edition** . . . welcome to romance.

Last year, I requested your opinions on the books that we publish. Thank you for the many thoughtful comments. For the next few months, I'd like to share quotes with you from those letters. This seems very appropriate while we are in the midst of the THAT SPECIAL WOMAN! promotion. Each one of our readers is a **special** woman, as heroic as the heroines in our books.

Our THAT SPECIAL WOMAN! title for October is *On Her Own* by Pat Warren. This is a heroine to cheer for as she returns to her hometown and the man she never forgot.

Also in store for you in October is *Marriage Wanted,* the third book in Debbie Macomber's heartwarming trilogy, FROM THIS DAY FORWARD. And don't miss *Here Comes the Groom* by Trisha Alexander, a spin-off from her *Mother of the Groom.*

Rounding out the month are books from Marie Ferrarella, Elizabeth Bevarly and Elyn Day, who makes her Silhouette Debut as Special Edition's PREMIERE author.

I hope you enjoy this book, and all of the stories to come!

Sincerely,

Tara Gavin
Senior Editor

QUOTE OF THE MONTH:

"I'm the mother of six, grandmother of ten and a registered nurse. I work in a hospice facility and deal with death and dying forty hours a week. Romance novels, light and airy, are my release from the stress."

L. O'Donnell
Maine

ELYN DAY

A BED OF ROSES

Silhouette®

SPECIAL EDITION®

Published by Silhouette Books New York

America's Publisher of Contemporary Romance

Special thanks to Dee and her fold of inspiring writers for their invaluable support, Laurie for a great title, Mom and Dad for being themselves, and Shadow for all the long walks. And to Jack, who believed and insisted we buy a computer, I love you!

SILHOUETTE BOOKS
300 East 42nd St., New York, N.Y. 10017

A BED OF ROSES

ISBN: 0-373-09846-4

First Silhouette Books printing October 1993

Printed in the U.S.A.

ELYN DAY

grew up with a love for books and the written word. Her first job after graduating from high school was shelving books for the county library. Other interests include woodworking, photography, sewing, leather-crafting and "nature sports." A native Oregonian, she lives in Portland with her high school sweetheart/husband/best friend, and although her roots are firmly planted, she loves to travel and pursue the slightly daring. Her writing career actually got its start when she jumped from an airplane with her husband and sold an essay on their experience to the local newspaper!

A Letter from the Author

Dear Reader,

Ten years ago I read a newspaper article about the romance market and how "everyday folks" were "banging out stories in their kitchens and garages, in between trips to the mailbox to collect royalty checks." The whole scenario sounded ideal to someone who loved books, had always been intrigued with writing and was in desperate need of a career goal. Except that I'd never read a romance! I borrowed a grocery bag of them and began to research and write.

Apparently, I'd missed some vital piece of information in that article, because it wasn't as easy as I'd thought it would be. For the next four years I floundered at the typewriter while continuing to work as a photo-lab technician. My husband finally convinced me to join a community college professional novel-writing class, where page one of *A Bed of Roses* came into being.

It took another four years of trial and error, encouragement from family and fellow writers, who have become like family to me, and dogged determination, to revise and finish the manuscript. When my agent called to tell me that Silhouette was interested, I went into a pleasant state of shock. I hung up the phone and began jumping and screaming! I'm sure my cat thought I'd gone berserk.

I hope you derive as much pleasure from reading my story as I did in writing it. And thank you!

Sincerely,

Elyn Day

Chapter One

Dana felt like a defenseless animal about to walk into a trap as she stood in the open doorway of East Ridge Hospital's physical-therapy center Monday afternoon. She gripped the walker she needed for support, aware of the throbbing in her left knee. The equipment along the off-white walls gleamed at her. The small room's low ceiling and worn bottle green carpet was a far cry from the enormous facility she'd grown accustomed to at Saint Jude Hospital in southwest Portland. Hardly the place where a specialist in sports injuries—the best Oregon had to offer, according to her doctor—would choose to work, she thought with apprehension. But then she suspected Dr. Stewart would have told her just about anything to get her back into therapy after her third and final operation four days ago.

There was a low exercise platform across from her. The wall behind it was mirrored and she stared at her own dismal reflection. Her dark glasses were too large for her small, pale face and her wide, full lips were compressed into a harsh line. The thick raven hair that fell down her back in a mass of natural waves was dull and lifeless, making her look older than her twenty-nine years. She had lost a lot of weight since the accident and the turquoise sweats she wore hung loosely on her five-foot-seven frame. Suppressing a groan, she looked away.

In the center of the room a young amputee was learning to walk with his new prosthesis to the low, insistent beat of pop music on the sound system. A petite, auburn-haired woman, dressed casually in a pink-striped jumpsuit and looking not much older than her patient, coached and encouraged him to take another step. Dana saw the determination on the boy's face, the beads of sweat as he struggled with the seemingly impossible. Despair and pity swept through her, and again she averted her gaze.

Her attention was drawn to another low platform at the end of the room where a tall, athletically built man was helping an elderly woman into a wheelchair. The corded muscles in his tanned arms flexed taut beneath the short sleeves of his white cotton shirt as they supported the woman's weight. Khaki slacks hugged his lean, muscled thighs. He towered over the frail woman, yet his touch appeared gentle, his dark eyes compassionate in the hard planes of his face. A full mustache, a shade darker than his chestnut hair, partially concealed his mouth as he spoke to the woman, then lifted at one corner in a crooked, almost roguish, smile. As if he were flirting with his patient to put her at ease, Dana mused.

Without warning, his gaze shifted and she found herself the target of his smile. It did little to put *her* at ease. "I'll be with you in a moment," he said.

She gave what she hoped was a convincing smile in return. She had met and interviewed a lot of men in her six years as a journalist and wasn't easily intimidated. But she knew by Dr. Stewart's description that the man watching her now was to be her new physical therapist, and a lump of fear lodged in her throat.

She watched him wheel his patient from the room. With a heavy sigh, she closed her eyes and allowed her shoulders to sag. Her outward charade of courage drained her, but she was determined to let no one see just how frightened she was. She wanted no one's pity.

"Are you all right?" The deep masculine voice came from above her.

Dana brought her head up sharply. The dark-haired man stood looking down at her. He seemed taller, more intimidating up close. She had to tip her head far back to meet his gaze.

"I'm fine," she lied, forcing another smile. "It's just a headache."

"Is that why you're wearing the dark glasses?"

"The lights hurt my eyes," she lied a second time.

"I see."

His voice was low, noncommittal. Dana had the feeling he was studying her and it made her uncomfortable that she couldn't tell what he was thinking.

Then his mouth curved into a smile that transformed the rugged lines of his face into an expression that startled her with its charming good looks.

"I'm Michael Gordon," he said, extending his right hand, "director of the PT center."

Dana shifted her weight to her left arm and took his hand in hers. His grip was firm and warm and electric. She immediately released it and said, "I'm Dana Whitaker. I have a two o'clock appointment."

"Yes. I've already spoken with your doctor. If you'll follow me, I have a few questions to ask before we get started."

He moved to the first of three desks that extended from the wall to his left, his stride smooth and unhurried. With excruciating slowness, Dana followed. She eased herself into the chair at the end of the desk and clasped her hands in her lap to still their trembling.

"I've studied your file," Michael Gordon said, sitting down. "You've been through physical therapy before, so you know what it's all about."

"Yes." She was unable to keep the harshness from her voice. Her knee felt as if it were made of hot wires and broken glass, throbbing with a pain as constant as her heartbeat. Physical therapy meant more pain— endless sessions of torture that left her feeling weak and helpless.

He nodded, his smile rueful, and said, "The torture chamber."

Dana frowned. "Pardon me?"

"That's what you call it, isn't it?"

The look in his dark eyes dared her to deny it. Dana found his arrogance annoying. "It would seem that you and Dr. Stewart have discussed more than my medical record.''

''Your mental attitude is as important to me as your physical condition,'' he explained.

''Then I don't have to tell you that I think this is all a waste of time.''

''Yet you're here.''

His voice remained calm, his eyes steady, and again Dana got the feeling that he was challenging her. The muscles in her jaw tightened and tears of frustration threatened to humiliate her. ''I don't see that I had much choice.''

''There are always choices,'' he told her. ''You could use your disability to get sympathy and attention. It's easier to say 'I can't' than to confront your pain.''

Dana drew her shoulders back. ''I'm not about to give up,'' she said tersely. ''And I certainly don't want anyone's sympathy.''

''What *do* you want?''

His softly spoken question brought her up short. The tears she'd thought under control pressed at the corners of her eyes. She was thankful for the concealment of her shaded glasses. She looked down at the dark, curly hair on his forearms folded across the desk in front of him. His arms were strong. As were his hands—broad, with blunt fingers. If he'd been anything but a physical therapist, she might have found them appealing.

She lifted her gaze to meet his. ''I want my leg—my life—to be the way it was before the accident,'' she stated, her low, even tone presenting him with a challenge of her own.

He shook his head. "That's not possible. You're not the same person you were then."

Dana glared at his uncompromising features. "You have the tact of a grenade."

Some unidentifiable emotion flashed across his features, but his gaze remained steady. "I'm trying to be honest with you, Dana. Your life has been changed by your experience. You can use that experience in a positive way, or you can let it make your life miserable."

"What could I possibly find *positive* about having my knee mangled?"

"That's a question only you can answer."

How she hated him at that moment. It was easy for him to sit there, healthy and strong, and preach to her. It wasn't his life that had been turned upside down by someone else's carelessness. She had suffered with this wretched knee for five months, for God's sake!

She looked at the walker beside her—the steel frame that allowed her mobility, yet held her prisoner. "All I want," she told him, "is to be able to walk without that damn thing."

He nodded and pushed away from the desk. "That's all I wanted to hear." Standing, he glanced down at her sweatpants and said, "I'll need to examine your knee. Have you got a pair of shorts to change into? If I try pushing that elastic cuff up, it's going to cut off your circulation."

Without a word, Dana slid her thumbs into the waistband of her pants, and by shifting her weight from one side to the other, was able to work them down over her hips, revealing the matching turquoise shorts she wore underneath.

"Will these do?" she asked, looking up. She'd hoped to shock him a little with her boldness. What she hadn't counted on was the amusement that glinted in his dark eyes, or the wave of heat that swept through her.

"Good," he commented with a crooked smile. "You've come prepared."

On the contrary, Dana thought. She had come prepared for more pain, not the annoying way her body temperature kept fluctuating. "You're forgetting I've had a lot of practice," she replied, her voice lacking any attempt at humor.

"No, Dana, I haven't forgotten."

There it was again. That fleeting expression in his eyes, as if the door to his emotions had blown open for a fraction of a second. What was he feeling? Dana wondered. Pity? Kindness? She wanted neither from him.

Anger. Now there was a good, solid emotion. It took her mind off the pain.

"Let me help you with those," he said. He knelt in front of her and slipped the canvas shoes from her feet, then eased her sweatpants down and off. Dana clenched her teeth, humiliated at not being able to do a simple thing like undress herself without a great deal of effort. She focused her gaze on the top of her physical therapist's head and the way his dark chestnut hair, cut short at the sides, curled invitingly over the collar of his shirt.

She jerked and found herself staring into his eyes.

"Did I hurt you?" he asked.

"No, I . . . No." She was babbling. What in God's name had come over her? She looked at her sweat-pants clutched in his strong hands and swallowed. "I'm fine," she managed in a reasonably stable voice. She grasped her walker and stood. "Where do you want me?"

"On one of the exam tables over there," he told her.

There were three of them lined up against the far wall, each with a white curtain that could be pulled along a track in the ceiling for privacy. As she maneuvered the walker around and started toward the nearest one, she could feel him watching her. She felt exposed in her shorts, her pale legs ghostly white in the harsh overhead lighting. Her movements were slow and painful. She wanted to scream at him for seeing her awkwardness.

Long, embarrassing seconds later, she managed to pull herself onto the edge of the table, determined not to allow her helplessness to undermine her self-respect a second time. A stab of pain rewarded her effort, and she silently cursed her pride.

"Lie down on your back," he instructed.

His broad fingers circled her ankles and helped to lift her legs onto the table. She lay back and stared at the ceiling.

"First I'm going to examine the muscles around your knee," he explained. "Then I'll check your range of motion with a goniometer."

Dana gave a compliant, curt nod. She knew she was committed to going through with the examination, just as she knew that any prodding or manipulation of her leg was going to hurt.

His strong hands began to explore tender muscles and ligaments. He slid one hand under the back of her knee, and placing his other one low on her thigh, said, "Press down and count to three."

She tried. The effort brought tears to her eyes. The hand on her thigh shifted to another muscle.

"Again."

She pressed, clenching her teeth against the pain.

"Good. Now roll onto your stomach."

Out of the corner of her eye, she saw him produce a protractor-type device with arms extending from its axis. He positioned it against her leg, with the axis at her knee, and instructed her to bring her lower leg back toward her body as far as possible. He measured the flexibility of her injured joint, or the lack of it, her passive and active ranges of motion and her strength through resistance. The tests didn't take more than a few minutes, but to Dana it was an eternity.

"That should do it," he said at last. "How are you feeling?"

Her entire body trembled in weakness. "Fine," she muttered.

A smile tugged at the corners of his mouth. "Good."

His smugness irritated her and she started to sit up.

He put a restraining hand on her shoulder. "Relax for a minute while I make some notes in your file."

There was that irksome kindness again. But she didn't argue with him. Instead, she lay back and closed her eyes.

It was frustrating to be so out of condition. She was used to long hours on her feet, chasing down stories, conducting interviews, endless research, always with a deadline at her heels. Her endurance had been inexhaustible. But now, after months of being sedentary, even the slightest exertion tired her beyond belief.

Realizing she was close to falling asleep, she opened her eyes to see Michael standing at his desk with his back to her. She took advantage of the opportunity to observe him unnoticed.

He had a broad, strong back that tapered to a trim waist and lean hips. His firm buttocks and long, muscled legs were indicative of a man who exercised often. A cyclist perhaps, or a runner. Or maybe he was a weekend jock who tackled men half his size, then guzzled beer in front of the TV, she thought with ill grace.

He turned and approached the exam table with the fluent ease more typical of a dancer than a couch jock. He definitely wasn't the latter, she decided.

"The exercises I'm going to start you on are relatively easy," he told her. "You're probably already familiar with most of them. Let's move to one of the mats and I'll go over them with you."

Dana took his hand and scooted off the exam table. Her left foot touched the floor first and a stab of pain greeted her. She gave a soft moan and shifted her weight to her right leg, only to have it buckle beneath her. Michael's arm was around her waist in an instant, and she found herself crushed against his chest.

He was strong and hard and very masculine. His body radiated heat. The unexpected contact made the breath catch in her throat. She stared at his chin and tried to remind herself that the man she was clinging to was her PT.

"Are you all right?"

She felt the words vibrate up his chest and brush her forehead. She lifted her gaze and looked into his eyes. They were the color of dark chocolate.

She swallowed and managed a nod.

"Put your arm around my waist," he said.

He's my therapist, she told herself again. But somehow she wasn't quite able to ignore the fact that he was also a very attractive man.

And she was staring at him like an idiot.

She jerked her gaze back down to his chin and slid her arm around his waist. If he drank beer, she thought crazily, it was in definite moderation. There wasn't an ounce of fat beneath the crisp fabric of his shirt.

"I imagine you're used to women throwing themselves at you," she commented in an attempt to make light of her embarrassment.

His deep chuckle reverberated through her. "I never looked at it that way before."

Dana met the amusement in his eyes with a wry smile. "You've probably never fallen into your PT's arms before either."

"No." He grinned. "I can't say I have."

She felt the warmth of his gaze clear to her toes and looked away, perturbed.

If he noticed, he didn't show it. He reached out and drew her walker closer. "Let's get started on those exercises."

For the next thirty minutes he supported and guided her leg, explaining the purpose of each movement and how it would help strengthen the muscles around her injured knee. Then he showed her exercises to do at home. They were simple, gentle movements that she had tried before with disappointing results. A feeling of helpless futility seized her and refused to let go. By the time he was finished, she was in a furious struggle with pain and angry frustration.

He brought her sweatpants and shoes over, but before he could help her, she grabbed them from him and stated, "I can manage. Thank you."

She thought she saw the corners of his mouth twitch, but he stood his ground and didn't argue. Dana clenched her teeth and fought back tears as she struggled to dress under his watchful gaze. She felt like a lab rat—a pathetic one, at that. After what seemed an eternity, she got her shoes on and pulled herself to her feet. She half expected some comment from him on her performance.

Instead, he said, "Exercise your leg as often as you can. It's important to keep those muscles flexible." Then he turned and walked to his desk. "I want to see you in here three days a week, same time, if that's possible."

As if I had anywhere else to be. She was unable to quell her bitterness. She'd been down this road before, too many times. "For how long?" she asked.

"For as long as it takes."

He was bent over his desk, writing. His apparent dismissal fueled her frustration and anger. "In other words, you don't know."

He laid his pen down and turned. Dana took small pleasure in the peeved expression etched on his face. She'd managed to breach his calm exterior, but she wasn't sure she liked the way he regarded her, his deep brown eyes narrowed, as if seeing through her dark glasses.

"I don't have the answers you want, Dana. How long this takes is up to you. You just haven't figured that out yet." He moved closer. "Are there any other questions?"

"No."

"Good. I'll escort you to the elevator."

"That won't be necessary." Dana turned her walker toward the door. "I can find my own way out. Good day, Mr. Gordon."

She was almost to the door when he called her name. She stopped and turned back toward him. He was a striking man, she had to admit, but something in his uncompromising stance made her wary.

"Yes?"

"I expect your headache to be gone by Wednesday," he said. "If not, take a couple of aspirin, but leave the glasses at home."

Dana's back stiffened. "Will that be all, Mr. Gordon?"

"We're going to be seeing a lot of each other. I would appreciate it if you would call me Michael."

Dana could think of a lot of things to call him at the moment. *Michael* was not one of them. Without giving him the satisfaction of a reply, she turned and left the room.

Michael watched Dana's painful exit—he could tell by the rigid way she held her back what the effort cost her—before easing his six-foot-one frame into the chair behind his desk. He stared at the open file in front of him and recalled something his friend Adam Stewart had said when he'd phoned last Friday.

"She refuses to go back to the PTs here at Saint Jude. She says they're all incompetent."

"She's scared," had been Michael's response. He'd seen it before. According to the history Adam had given him, she'd been through a hell of a lot. Two unsuccessful corrective surgeries and finally a pin implant just last week. And in between operations, a lot of physical therapy. She'd spent the past five months in pain, facing one disappointment after another.

"What makes you think she'll see me?"

"I'll tell her you're the best in your field," had been Adam's reply.

"You think she'll buy that?"

"Why shouldn't she? It's the truth. Why you're hiding your talent at East Ridge, I'll never understand. You were making good money here."

"You know the money doesn't mean anything to me." At thirty-six, Michael had all he needed in material things. Sure, the facilities were limited at East Ridge—it was a small, community hospital—but he knew he could do more good here than he ever could in a larger hospital. Working at Saint Jude had left him feeling oppressed and overwhelmed by a maze of administration. Los Angeles General all over again. The only good thing to come out of his year at Saint Jude was his friendship with Dr. Adam Stewart.

"Mike, if this is going to cause a problem—"

"Don't worry about it. I'll be glad to do what I can."

Michael only hoped that Dana could hold on to her stubbornness in the weeks to follow. If she stopped believing she would ever walk without a crutch of some kind, then it wouldn't matter how well her knee healed or how extensive her therapy was. The mind could be as powerful as the most advanced medicine. He thought of her wide, full lips pressed together in determination and the willful tilt of her delicate chin. For some reason, it brought a smile to his face.

"She's one feisty lady."

Michael blinked and looked up at Sally, his young assistant PT, standing beside the desk. She had a funny smirk on her small, round face.

"What did you say?"

Sally pointed at the file. "Your new patient. I said, she's one feisty lady. But what's with the dark glasses?"

"It's a defense mechanism to keep people from seeing how she's really feeling," he explained. "A sign of denial that anything's wrong."

"Mmm...that's a shame. She might be pretty without those awful things hiding half her face."

Michael saw the teasing glint in Sally's hazel eyes. "She's a patient," he reminded her.

An attractive one, he admitted to himself. She was hurting physically and emotionally, but there was fire in her, a stubbornness of spirit that was encouraging—and charming.

Not that that had anything to do with anything. He wasn't looking for involvement. Especially with a patient. He was a professional. He never used the patient-therapist relationship, or the close physical contact necessary in that oftentimes-love/hate alliance, to approach or intimidate a person in his care.

Sally perched her bottom on the corner of his desk, dangling her stocking-clad feet next to him. The casual observer might have thought she was flirting with him, but Michael knew better. Sally liked to make herself comfortable wherever she happened to be.

"In the six months that you've been here, I've never seen you so much as look twice at a woman," she commented. "Why is that?"

Michael enjoyed the comfortable relationship he had with his co-worker, but their friendship did not extend beyond the hospital. "That's my business," he told her, not unkindly.

"I'm sorry. I didn't mean to be nosy." She chewed at her lower lip for a second, then leaned closer and asked in a subdued voice, "You're not gay, are you?"

The corners of Michael's mouth twitched. "What would you do if I said yes?"

A pitiful expression puckered her face and she replied, "I'd mourn for the women of the world."

Michael threw his head back and laughed.

"Seriously, Michael, if I were ten years older and not happily engaged—"

"Now you're calling me old!" He shook his head in feigned remorse. "I think you'd better see to your next patient before you do any more damage to my ego."

Sally laughed and slid to her feet. But before she moved away, she gave Dana Whitaker's file a flick with her finger. "It can't hurt to look, huh?"

Michael regarded her retreating back with an uncomfortable feeling growing in the pit of his stomach. Dana Whitaker was fragile and vulnerable. She possessed an underlying strength that challenged him. But that wasn't the cause of his unease.

He looked back down at the file. Everything was there—the surgeries, the bouts with depression, the setbacks. But it was his new patient's occupation that caught and held his attention. The feeling in his stomach twisted.

Journalist.

It surprised him how that one word could still stir painful memories.

He closed the file.

He'd dedicated his life to helping people regain the use of their bodies after an injury or illness and he wasn't about to turn his back on that now, any more than he'd let his friend Adam down.

He would treat Dana Whitaker like any other patient, and forget for the time being that a reporter had damn near destroyed his career.

Chapter Two

Last week's showers had given way to a spell of un-
seasonably warm weather for mid-May. The afternoon sun beat down on Dana as she waited outside the
hospital for Peter. He was late again. She squinted
down the street for a glimpse of his ugly green hatch-
back. The sunlight bouncing off chrome and steel
made her head throb. She was dressed too warmly and
her skin prickled beneath her sweats.

"Darn it, Peter." She didn't like being dependent
upon others for things she used to do for herself, and
Peter's recently developed habit of keeping her waiting grated on her nerves.

"I have a quick errand to run," he'd told her when
he'd dropped her off over an hour ago.

They'd met at the *Multnomah County Gazette*
where they both worked—he as a photographer, she

as a feature writer. She'd admired his mild mannered, easygoing style and his ability to capture a subject with one perfectly composed photo. With his pictures and her words they'd made a team. Dana knew that there were others on the newsroom staff who'd expected the relationship to go further, but she'd learned through experience that work and romance weren't compatible. Peter had made a token advance, which she had politely, but firmly, turned down. With that out of the way, they'd settled into a comfortable working friendship.

Confident that the accident was a temporary setback, Peter had offered to chauffeur Dana to her doctor visits and PT sessions. Their editor, Valerie Evans, gave him leeway to adjust his schedule accordingly. But after five months and no end in sight, her disability had become an inconvenience.

Dana found herself wishing her parents were around. It was a selfish thought that she immediately pushed aside. They were in Europe, on a vacation they'd been planning for a long time and had postponed because of her accident. Plagued by guilt, she'd finally convinced them that she was well enough to look after herself. Still, they rescheduled their trip only after Steven, her older brother, had promised to keep an eye on her while they were away. He'd be here now if she hadn't assured him that everything was taken care of.

When Peter's car finally turned into the parking lot, relief, anger and apprehension swept through Dana. Marla Wright, the pretty blond journalist who also worked at the *Gazette,* was sitting in the front seat.

Dana had been with the *Gazette* for almost two years when Marla was hired. The new reporter had proven herself energetic, dauntless, sometimes ruthless in her methods. She was a good writer and her looks got her into places where other reporters had the door slammed in their faces. But it was her resentment of Dana's friendship with the paper's editor, making accusations that Dana got the best assignments because of it, that stirred the rivalry between them.

Peter pulled up to the curb and got out. His tweed jacket hung open and his tie was loosely knotted over a blue pin-striped shirt. A light breeze tousled his short wheat-colored hair. "Sorry I'm late," he said, coming around the car. "I went back to check a photo layout and lost track of the time."

"You've been gone for almost an hour and a half," Dana grumbled.

His step faltered and a frown creased his long, angular face, but before he had a chance to respond, Marla emerged from the car.

"Dana! How are you?" she asked smoothly, her ice blue eyes taking in Dana's appearance with a quick, careless sweep. Her shoulder-length ash blond hair framed the delicate features of her face. She wore a coral body-hugging knit dress that scooped low at the neckline and stopped well above her knees. White slingbacks clung to her dainty feet. She was not only graceful and pretty, but also five years younger than Dana.

"Marla," Dana acknowledged.

"I hope you don't mind that I came along," the younger woman said, her sunny coral lips curving in an ingratiating smile, "but Peter and I have a story to cover, and it was easier on him this way."

The intentional dig hit its mark. Dana felt her self-esteem plummet to new depths.

Peter thrust his hands into the pockets of his beige tweed slacks, their customary place when they weren't wrapped around a camera, and asked, "So how'd it go?"

Dana looked into his gray eyes and wondered if he really cared. "I'd rather not talk about it right now."

Peter's frown deepened. "What's wrong, Danny? Did something happen in there to upset you?"

I'm upset because everything is wrong with my life! her mind screamed. *Can't you see that? It should be me going with you, not this... this... fashion statement!* She gave a sigh of exasperation and shook her head. "I'm hot and I'm tired. That's all."

"Then get in and let me take you home."

The caring in his voice melted Dana's resolve to be angry with him. She nodded and gave him a half-hearted smile. He helped her into the front seat, then took her walker to the rear of the car and began wrestling it in around his camera equipment. Marla took the back seat. Long minutes later, Peter muttered a curse and slammed the hatch door shut. Dana closed her eyes and pressed her fingers to her temples. She would take a hot bath and a nap, she promised herself, and things wouldn't look as bleak. She clung to this thought as Peter climbed in and started the car's engine.

The atmosphere was oppressive, and a strained silence fell over the threesome. Dana searched for something to talk about, but her ability to make trivial conversation—like so many other things she'd once done without thinking—no longer existed. She glanced over at Peter. The sharp angles of his jaw stood out in relief and a nerve ticked in his cheek. She didn't like what her disability was doing to their friendship, but she didn't seem to have any control over it. Michael Gordon had been brutally honest when he'd said that her life would never be the same as it had been before the accident.

Remembering her new PT produced an odd queasy feeling in her stomach. It hadn't gone well between them, and she knew she was at least partly to blame. She turned her head and gazed out the window at a city in bloom—fragrant lilacs, crimson rhododendron, purple azaleas, delicate pink and white fuchsia. The smell of newly mowed grass, green and crisp, filled the air. They passed a Tri-Met station where two teenage girls, wearing skintight spandex pants and long baggy shirts, waited for the bus. Dana envied their animated conversation and their youth.

Tall evergreens on a manicured grassy slope marked the entrance to the Grotto. Dana breathed a little easier, knowing she was almost home. Through the trees, she could make out the massive stone church and the elevator tower that clung to the rocky cliff behind it. She longed for the serene walks she used to take through the landscaped grounds above.

Peter steered the car into her long, graveled driveway. The small two-bedroom house, painted a soft green, with white shutters and trim, sat back from the road, nestled in a stand of fir trees. Waist-high azalea bushes, blanketed in scarlet blooms, lined the walk that led from the double garage to the front door.

Peter drove up to the side entrance and stopped. "Here we are."

"What a quaint little house," Marla commented.

Dana made no reply as she searched through her purse for her keys.

Peter got out and went around to the back of the car for her walker. Dana sensed Marla's cool eyes watching from the back seat, then heard her even cooler voice.

"I hope you appreciate all that Peter has done for you."

Dana made a fist around her keys. "That's not your concern," she replied, struggling to keep her own voice neutral.

Marla waited until Peter had slammed the hatch shut again before continuing, "I've seen the way you've been using him, and I think it's a shame."

The younger woman's words had the sting of truth. Dana's shoulders stiffened. "You would know, wouldn't you, Marla?"

"What do you mean by that?"

Dana sighed. She didn't have the strength or the will for a verbal sparring match. "Nothing. Forget I said anything."

Peter opened the car door and, to Dana's great relief, Marla shut up.

"Ready?" he asked. His gaze flicked from her to Marla, then back.

"Yes." She took his hand and let him help her out of the car.

"Goodbye, Dana," Marla called lightly.

Dana ignored her. Grasping her walker, she started toward the house.

"When do you go back for therapy again?" Peter asked, walking beside her.

She waited until he'd unlocked the door for her and returned her keys, before answering. "I'm not sure."

"What do you mean? Didn't you make another appointment?"

Dana looked up at him. "I mean I'm not sure I want you to take me."

His lips compressed. "I said I was sorry about being late."

"If you're tired of being my chauffeur, say so," Dana challenged. "Don't make this any harder for me than it already is."

Peter thrust his hands into his pockets. "Do you think it's been easy for me, juggling my time between you and my job?" he asked.

"No, Peter, I don't. That's why I think it's time I started doing things for myself."

"That's crazy. How will you get around?" he demanded.

"I'm a big girl. I'll manage."

His gaze narrowed. "Did Marla say something to you?"

Dana gave her head a sad shake. "She has nothing to do with it. Face it, Peter, you and I both know it wasn't supposed to go on this long. Let's call it good while we're still on speaking terms, okay?"

"No, it's not okay. How will you get around?"

"I'll call Steven."

She could see he was torn between duty and freedom. "I feel like I'm abandoning you," he admitted.

"You're my partner, not my baby-sitter."

"I wish." His mouth took on a wry twist. "This new PT didn't say when you could come back to work, did he?"

"No." A feeling of impotent frustration made the word sound harsher than she'd intended.

"I'm sorry, Danny. I know how hard this is for you. I just wish—"

The car horn interrupted him with two short blasts. Marla had moved to the front seat and was watching them with a perturbed expression marring her lovely face.

"You'd better not keep her waiting," Dana said.

Peter frowned, still unsure. "You'll call me if there's anything you need?"

She nodded. "Thanks, but I'll be fine," she assured him. Maneuvering the walker around, she turned and went inside.

Dana was dragged from sleep by the insistent ringing of the telephone next to her ear. Disoriented, she glanced at the bedside clock as she reached for the receiver.

Eight-thirty? She glanced over her shoulder at the lace-covered window and the darkness beyond, and realized she'd slept through the afternoon. She had gone straight to bed after Peter had dropped her off, too exhausted mentally as well as physically to contend with taking a bath. The aspirin she had taken before lying down had worn off, and her leg ached.

"Hello?" she muttered, her voice still heavy with sleep.

"Did I wake you?" It was Valerie.

"Yes," Dana grumbled, attempting to sound put-out. But it was good to hear her friend's voice. She pulled herself up and leaned against the carved pine headboard. The movement brought the pain in her leg into sharp awareness and she gave an involuntary moan.

"Are you all right?" Valerie asked.

Dana massaged her temple. "If one more person asks me that, I will scream."

She heard Val's low chuckle. "I take it you haven't had a good day?"

"You know me and physical therapy. I'd rather have a tooth pulled."

"Is this new therapist as good as Dr. Stewart made him out to be?"

Dana shifted uncomfortably. She'd been trying not to think about him. "He seemed competent enough," she replied. *And arrogant and damned good-looking.*

"Go on," Valerie coaxed. "What did he say?"

"Nothing I haven't heard before."

"Why do I get the feeling you don't want to talk about it?"

"I'm sorry," Dana muttered. "It just seems like that's all I talk about anymore. My life has become an endless rerun of surgery and physical therapy. I'm tired of it."

"I know, Danny. Your life hasn't exactly been a bed of roses lately. I'm as anxious to see you on your feet again as you are. You're missed around here."

Dana felt guilty knowing her absence meant more work for the other journalists. At least she was able to help by handling the special sections of the *Gazette*— seasonal activities, home-improvement articles, human-interest stories. With the Portland Rose Festival only three weeks away, there was plenty to do. The month-long celebration covered a wide array of events, from the arrival of over a dozen naval vessels on the Willamette River, to a fun center with rides and food booths, spectacular parades, and a fifteen-kilometer race through downtown Portland.

She worked on her home computer, doing most of her research over the telephone. Specials took longer to prepare than other sections of the weekly paper and were usually doled out to the journalists on top of their regular duties.

She'd also been writing cutlines for Peter's photos, but she wouldn't be surprised if Marla took over that job, as well. "Are you still at the paper at this hour?" she asked, irritated by the sullenness of her thoughts.

Valerie made a derisive sound. "Where else would I be?"

"Home feeding L.B." Lover Boy was an overweight orange cat that had wandered into Valerie's life about a year ago. Dana thought it was a shame that at thirty-nine and holding, her friend had yet to find a man who was willing to conform to the busy life of an editor. Then she thought of her own luck with men and wondered if maybe she shouldn't get a pet.

"That cat could stand to miss a meal or two," Val commented.

"Don't let him hear you say that!"

Valerie laughed. "He'd disown me for sure." Then she gave an audible sigh. "I've got to get back to work. I just called to see how you were doing and ask if there was anything I could get for you."

"Thanks, but I'll be fine." Maybe if she said it often enough she'd start believing it.

"I'll come by later in the week," Val promised.

"That would be great."

Dana hung up the phone and flipped on the brass reading lamp next to the bed. The soft glow of the low-watt bulb teased the room's peach-tone walls and secondhand furniture—a tall, pine dresser and a cane rocker, compliments of her mom and dad. The nightstands were inexpensive bookcases she'd assembled from a kit, their white-lacquered shelves crammed with paperback novels, mostly mysteries. The only new piece in the room was the double bed, a luxury she'd treated herself to.

She tossed back the peach comforter and slipped out of the teddy-bear pajama top she wore. Grabbing her walker, she made her way the short distance down the hall to the bathroom.

A lot of things that she had done with automatic ease before her accident had become exercises in endurance. Soaking in a hot bath was one of them. She sat on the edge of the tub, the white porcelain like a block of ice against her bare skin, and turned on the water. She was chilled to the bone by the time the tub was full. Grasping the hand bar that Steven had installed for her, she swung her right leg into the hot water. Keeping her injured leg propped on the edge, she carefully began lowering herself into the tub.

Her hand slipped. She whacked her elbow on the tub's edge and landed on her bottom, hard. Bathwater sloshed onto the blue tiled floor.

"Dammit!" she cried. She struck the wall with the side of her fist. Tears blurred her vision and she hit the wall again. Depression had become her tormentor, a foe she was in constant battle with to suppress. Weary of fighting it, she put her face in her hands and sobbed unrestrained.

She hated this feeling of helplessness and inability. She hated self-pity, but still she found herself asking "Why me?" If she hadn't stayed so long at the benefit Christmas party she'd been covering, maybe she wouldn't have been in the intersection when the driver of the other car had run the red light. He'd plowed into the side of her Volkswagen Beetle with his big sedan. She learned later that he'd been drinking, coming home from a party of his own. He survived the accident unscathed, while she was left with a leg that might never function properly again. Some Christmas!

She gazed at her leg propped on the edge of the tub. The ten-inch-long incision with its ugly black stitches was puffy and angry looking. The image of Marla Wright's shapely legs flashed before her. A sob escaped her lips and she looked away.

She splashed water on her face and lay back in the tub, closing her red, swollen eyes. Without warning, Michael Gordon's dark good looks appeared in her thoughts, and her heart picked up its pace. There was nothing weak about the man. She remembered with stark clarity the feeling of his strong arms around her and his lean, muscled body pressed against hers. Its impact on her had been disturbing. She didn't want to like him. His physical presence made her all the more aware of her own weakness and vulnerability. His deep masculine voice provoked her anger.

But most of all, he frightened her. He would expect her to do things she wasn't capable of. He'd coax, push, encourage and badger her, just as her previous physical therapists had done. The thought of going back terrified her.

And yet she couldn't give up. The thought of going through the rest of her life in her present condition terrified her even more. To quit now would be to mock the independent, strong-willed woman she had fought so hard to become.

She had assured Michael Gordon that she would not give up, and she wouldn't. But she would do it for herself—not because she cared what some good-looking, overbearing physical therapist might think of her.

Chapter Three

Steven came over the following morning. Dana was in the kitchen attempting to get around with her walker and make a pot of coffee at the same time, when she heard the familiar sound of his four-wheel-drive pickup approach the house. She dropped the coffee filter and its contents onto the counter and managed to reach the door as he was about to knock.

"Hey, sis, how're you doing?"

At an even six feet, he was five inches taller than Dana, his high cheekbones and wide expressive mouth more masculine versions of her soft features. He wore a jade chamois shirt and black slacks, his short-cropped raven hair neatly combed away from his face. Blue-green eyes, the same shade as his sister's, looked down at her thoughtfully.

Dana smiled. "Hey, yourself. Don't just stand there, come in."

He stepped inside and closed the door. "You haven't answered my question."

"I'm fine."

"Look at me when you say that, and maybe I'll believe you."

Dana held her breath and met his gaze.

His dark brows dipped. "Sit down and tell me what's going on."

"Honestly, Steven—"

"Don't argue with your big brother." He grinned and turned away from the face she made at him. Grabbing the sponge at the edge of the sink, he began cleaning up the spilled coffee grounds.

Although painted bright white with sunny yellow accents to give the illusion of size, the kitchen was too small to comfortably accommodate two cooks at once, especially when one of them used a bulky walker and wasn't very adept with it. Dana sat out of the way at the small dinette in the corner and watched as Steven salvaged the filter and measured fresh grounds. Making coffee was one of the few things her brother knew how to do in the kitchen.

"Why aren't you at work?" she asked.

"I've got a one o'clock flight to catch," he answered over his shoulder. "Cascade Machine is sending me to Phoenix to do some troubleshooting for a big industrial plant down there."

He poured the last of the water into the coffeemaker and turned around before Dana could hide the disappointment on her face. His frown returned.

"Suppose you tell me what's wrong," he said, sitting across the table from her.

"I was going to call you later and ask you to take me to therapy tomorrow." She went on to explain why Peter was no longer her chauffeur. "After all, he can't program the news to coincide with my schedule," she said. "And he has a life of his own."

"I wish you'd told me sooner."

Dana gave a shrug of nonchalance she didn't feel. "I'll just make other arrangements." At the moment, though, she couldn't have said what those arrangements might be.

Steven shook his head. "I'll tell the boss to send somebody else."

Even though she knew it wasn't intended to be taken that way, Dana found his remark a bit too self-sacrificing, and it annoyed her. She was fed up with feeling like a burden to her family and friends. "You'll do no such thing," she stated, her tone firm. "I'm not an invalid."

"I never said you were, sis. But the reality is, there are still some things you can't do for yourself—like drive a car."

"And you have a job to do," she reminded him. "Stop worrying about me, Steven. You're talking to a resourceful journalist, remember?" She shot him a mischievous smile and added, "My thumb still works." She demonstrated by sticking it in the air as if she were hitching a ride.

Steven scowled. "That's not even remotely funny."

"I was only teasing," Dana insisted.

"Well, I'm not. How do you intend to get to therapy? And what if you fall or something and need to get to the hospital? You know Mom and Dad will have my neck if anything happens to you."

"After they find out I've had surgery again without telling them, I don't think *you'll* have anything to worry about," Dana commented dryly. She wasn't looking forward to telling them that she'd been scheduled for the pin implant before they left and had kept quiet about it. She hadn't even told Steven until their parents' plane had taken off.

"I'm serious, sis."

Dana gave a resigned sigh. "I'll call Val, all right?"

Her brother considered this for a second, then nodded. "All right. I'll only be gone a couple of days," he assured her. "And I'll call you the minute I get back."

"Good. Now, how about some of that coffee?"

When he left an hour later to catch his flight, Dana felt abandoned. Despite her reassurances that she could manage without him, a lump formed in her throat as she watched his pickup back out of the driveway.

She put off calling Val until it was too late. The truth of the matter was, she didn't want to be a bother to her friend. She tried to talk herself out of going to physical therapy entirely.

And yet she couldn't ignore the accusing little voice in her head. *You know if you miss this once, you'll never go back. Is that what you want?*

An hour before her scheduled appointment Wednesday afternoon, she jammed her dark glasses on her nose and called a cab.

* * *

Michael was supervising Sally's work with a young man recovering from neck trauma when an odd tingling at the back of his own neck made him turn. Dana Whitaker stood watching him from across the room. Despite her dark glasses, he knew he was the target of her gaze by the thin line of her mouth. She'd made it quite clear on her previous visit to the center that she didn't intend to like him. Apparently she hadn't changed her mind.

He'd thought about that face often, much to his annoyance. His curiosity to know what lay hidden behind the defensive shields had become something of a challenge. He'd tried imagining different eye colors and sizes and shapes, but nothing seemed to fit her. He'd forgotten how vulnerable she looked even with the glasses. And stubborn. He had to admire her guts.

She wore mint-colored sweats today and he wondered with mild amusement if she had shorts to match them, as well. But he was careful to keep his expression neutral as he walked toward her. She was testing him. If he failed the test, he failed her.

Dana watched him approach and wished she'd stayed home. The short-sleeved azure knit shirt he wore complemented his muscular shoulders, and a pair of blue jeans, beginning to show wear, hugged his narrow hips and long legs. But it was the scowl on his rugged face that made her heart pound in her chest. It took all of her willpower not to back away from him.

"I told you to leave the glasses at home," he said in an even voice.

Her hands tightened on the walker and she met his uncompromising gaze. "I told you the lights hurt my eyes."

"Bull."

Dana couldn't believe she'd heard him right. "What?" she sputtered.

He leaned forward and put his hands on her walker, bringing his face down to her level. Dana's senses registered the warmth of his breath and the faint scent of his musky after-shave. The look in his dark eyes sent a shiver through her. They were too direct. Too discerning. As if he could see through her defenses and into her soul.

"I can't treat you if you don't let me see what you're feeling, Dana."

Her gaze dropped to his restraining hands so close to hers. "Let me go."

"Everyone cries," he continued. "There's nothing wrong with letting that show."

Dana felt trapped. He was asking too much. It was wrong to let her tears show. To cry was to admit to the pain. And to admit to the pain was to admit her helplessness. She felt the tears she hated welling in her eyes.

"I said, let me go," she repeated, her voice stronger this time.

Michael could feel her trembling through the frame of the walker. Was it fear or anger? he wondered. God, how he hated playing the tough guy. But letting her have her way would accomplish nothing. He knew if he gave in to her now he'd never be able to work with her.

"You can't stand to be out of control, can you?" he persisted. "I'm holding the walker, not you. You're free to leave any time."

She brought her head up sharply. "Damn you, I can't!"

Out of the corner of his eye, Michael saw Sally leave her patient at the stationary bicycle and come toward them.

"It's all right," he said with a dismissive glance. Sally hesitated, then returned to her patient without argument.

He looked back at Dana—what he could see of her. She was chewing at her lower lip as if she'd just lost her last friend.

"This is more than a job to me," he told her, "and I'll do whatever it takes to help you. But you're going to have to meet me halfway. I'm not asking you to like me, Dana, but I do need your trust." He released her walker and straightened. "I won't lie to you about your condition. You deserve my honesty, not my sympathy." He stood with his arms hanging loose at his sides and regarded her. There was nothing left to say, he decided. It was up to her to make the next move.

Seconds seemed to drag into minutes. Then something in her expression changed. With unsteady fingers, she slowly reached up and removed the glasses.

Michael was struck by the incredible color of her eyes. Maybe it was the green in her sweatshirt that made them look so intense, like clear emeralds on blue velvet. He knew now why he hadn't been able to imagine their color. He'd never seen such a color before. It fit her.

A single tear slid down her cheek and she swiped at it with the palm of her hand. "All right, Mr. Gordon..." She stopped, her lips compressed. "Michael," she corrected. "We'll do it your way."

She wasn't used to giving in. That she saw it as a defeat, rather than a compromise, troubled Michael. So did the sound of his name coming from her lips, but he'd worry about that later. "I wish I could make you understand," he said. "When you fight me, you defeat yourself."

She looked down at the dark glasses clasped in her hand. "It's not you I'm fighting," she admitted tightly. "It's the pain."

Michael knew what it cost her. She was a fighter, all right. It went against her nature to admit she was frightened and hurting.

He realized she was also beginning to trust him. "Let me help you do something about it," he softly challenged.

Her chin came up and she leveled her gaze to his. "You said you wouldn't lie to me about my condition. Do you feel I have a chance for a full recovery?"

"Yes."

He answered without hesitation and she smiled—the first genuinely honest smile he'd seen from her. It offered him a glimpse of the carefree woman she'd been before the accident.

And would be again, he vowed. He couldn't explain why it was so important to him, other than that it was his job. "Shall we get started?" he asked.

Dana nodded and maneuvered her walker toward the nearest exercise mat, her hampered movements a stark reminder of the long weeks of hard work that lay ahead of them.

When Michael emerged from the hospital an hour and a half later, he saw a familiar figure standing at the edge of the sidewalk in front of the building. A frown of concern pulled at his brows as he approached her. "Dana?"

She turned. She wore her dark glasses against the late-afternoon sun, but he could see the weariness in the lines around her mouth.

"Is anything wrong?" he asked.

"My cab is late."

It was more than simple annoyance in her voice, Michael realized. The woman was worn-out. It was evident in the way she leaned against her walker, as if without it she would collapse.

Why was she taking a cab to therapy? Where were her family? Her friends? Adam had mentioned a brother. Where the hell was he? The thought that she might have been left to face this latest challenge alone sent a surge of anger through Michael.

"Do you take a cab to therapy often?" he asked, careful not to let his anger show in his voice.

"Just today. My ride...fell through." Dana looked away. It was one more glaring testimony to her dependence on others. The fact that this man was her PT and would be sympathetic to her dilemma didn't make it any easier. She didn't want his sympathy. She wanted the damn cab.

"It's not as if East Ridge is hard to find," Michael offered. "Maybe the driver has had mechanical problems. Would you like me to go inside and give the company a call?"

Dana felt a weight drop in her stomach. "What did you say?"

"I asked if you'd like me to—"

"No," she interrupted, shaking her head. "You said something about East Ridge...." Her sentence faded away as the realization of her mistake took shape. The weight in her stomach became a leaden mass. "I told the dispatcher I was at Saint Jude Hospital," she groaned. "How could I be so stupid?"

"Don't be too hard on yourself, Dana. It was an easy mistake to make."

Easy for him, maybe. He wasn't the one who'd been waiting for a cab that was never coming. She rubbed her temple and fought back the urge to sit down and cry.

"Let me go inside and call the cab company," Michael said. "Then I'll give you a ride home."

Dana knew he was trying to help. After all, it was his job. But it only made her feel more helpless. She drew her shoulders back and sucked in a deep, steadying breath. "Thank you, but I couldn't ask you to do that."

"You didn't. I offered."

"I don't want to impose," she argued.

"It's no imposition. You're dangerously close to exhaustion, Dana. I'd feel better knowing you got home safely."

She felt a wry smile tug at her mouth as she tilted her head and regarded him. "I thought you were my physical therapist, not my doctor."

He grinned. "Close enough."

Maybe it was his perfect row of teeth and the way his dark eyes danced. Or maybe he was right and she was simply too exhausted to argue with him anymore. Whatever the reason, she gave a small smile and said, "All right, I accept."

He drove a white BMW convertible. Dana sank into the richly upholstered bucket seat and luxuriated in the way it cradled her body. She laid her head back against the rest and felt the warmth of the sun on her face and the wind tugging at her long black hair.

But knowing Michael sat in the seat next to her made it difficult to relax completely. He drove with an easy confidence, his hands firm and sure on the wheel, as he followed the directions she gave him.

No. It was the man, not his driving, that made her uncomfortable. She'd discovered it was a lot easier to be nice to him than she'd thought.

She studied him from the corner of her eye. He had a strong profile—determined—intelligent—uncompromising. But there was kindness in the lines of his tanned features, also. She'd witnessed it at unexpected moments in the PT center. The wind swept his chestnut hair away from a broad forehead. His nose was straight and not too long. His mouth was a mystery, partially hidden beneath his trimmed mustache. She'd never kissed a man with a mustache before.

He turned and smiled at her. Dana felt the heat rise in her cheeks.

"Comfortable?" he asked.

Not in the least, she thought. She swallowed hard and did her best to return his smile. "How could I be otherwise?" She ran a caressing hand over the edge of the soft tawny fabric that cushioned her ride and commented, "It's a beautiful car."

Michael turned his eyes back to the road, his smile gone. "It was my wife's."

Chapter Four

Michael clenched his jaw so hard his teeth hurt. What in God's name had possessed him to say *that?* The last thing he wanted to discuss was his wife, but it had been out of his mouth before he could stop it. He could feel Dana watching him.

"She...died," he explained. A cold familiar ache, one he had thought he was free of, gripped his heart.

Dana was stunned. "I'm sorry, Michael."

His gaze flicked to hers, then away. "Thank you." He gave a quick shrug and continued, "I'm coping. It's been almost two years." He braked for a red light. "A lifetime ago," he added, as if to himself.

Dana knew better. She could see the viselike grip he had on the steering wheel and the pained sadness in the tight muscles of his jaw. He must have loved his wife a great deal, she thought. She didn't understand why he had told her, but she was glad he had. It made him less intimidating. More human.

When he glanced her way again, his smile had returned, but a trace of sadness still lingered in his dark brown eyes. "What about you?" he asked. "Have you ever been married?"

Dana shook her head. In the few relationships she'd had with men, none had ever come close to being permanent. "I guess you could say I've been married to my career," she answered with a bland smile.

Michael's stomach lurched. Somehow he'd managed to forget who she was. What she was. "You're a reporter, is that right?" he asked, his voice expressionless.

"I'm a journalist for the *Multnomah County Gazette.*"

"Have you been doing that long?"

"I've been with the *Gazette* almost six years," she replied. "I majored in journalism in college and interned for the *Gresham Outlook* for a while. I also did some freelance work."

"What sorts of things do you write about?" Michael was finding it hard to talk around the tightness in his throat. Memories assaulted his brain, painful ones.

Dana gave a short laugh. "Anything and everything." She brushed at a strand of hair that the wind had whipped across her cheek. "For the most part, though, I write about people...human-interest stories. I'm a feature writer."

Michael's stomach took another abrupt slide.

Dana glanced over at him when he didn't say anything and was startled by the grim set of his mouth beneath his mustache. "Is something wrong?" she asked.

He fixed her with a look so fierce it made her cringe. A deep scowl furrowed his brow and his narrowed gaze impaled her. An instant later, recognition dawned in his expression, and he looked away.

"No," he muttered. "Nothing's wrong."

His lie hurt. Tears sprang to her eyes, stunning her. She furiously blinked them back. Why should it matter to her what he thought?

"Take a right at the next street," she said, her voice toneless.

Michael slowed the car and turned. He felt like an ass. "Dana, I—"

"It's the gravel drive at the end," she interrupted.

He pulled into the driveway of a tidy-looking green house surrounded by trees and shrubs. When he shut off the engine, the silence was immediate. "You have a nice place," he told her.

She replied with a curt "Thank you" that left him feeling at odds with himself. He'd wanted to apologize, but after a second's thought, decided it was better this way. He didn't want to have to make false excuses. And telling the truth was out of the question.

Dana dropped her sunglasses into her purse and pulled out her keys, while Michael got her walker.

"Thank you for the ride," she told him with polite coolness.

"You're welcome." He steadied the walker as she pulled herself to her feet. "Is transportation going to be a problem for you?"

"I'll manage." Dana resented the question. If Michael Gordon thought she was going to impose on him again, he had another think coming.

"Let me walk you to the door."

"No. I'll be fine."

Even as she said it, an overwhelming loneliness swept through her. She wasn't certain where it had come from, but by the time she reached the door to her house, her vision had begun to blur. She fumbled with the keys, desperate to get inside, but the lock swam before her tear-filled eyes. She knew Michael was watching from somewhere behind her and it made her all the more desperate.

The keys fell from her hand. She looked down at the indistinguishable lump at her feet and let out a helpless sob. She cursed her inability to do something as simple as stoop down to pick them up. She cursed her inability to control her seesawing emotions.

A shadow fell over her and she caught her breath as a dark shape retrieved her keys.

"Let me get those for you." Michael was beside her, holding the keys in his broad hand. He saw her tears. "What's wrong, Dana?"

She avoided his gaze, wishing she'd left her dark glasses on. She didn't want him to see her this way.

"Why are you crying?" he gently persisted. "Are you hurt?"

Yes! her mind screamed. But it wasn't her knee. She didn't know what it was. She couldn't think when he looked at her with such compassion in his expression. She closed her eyes and fought for control.

"Dana, talk to me."

A ragged breath shook her body. Damn him and his dogged determination to get inside her head! She opened her eyes, angry with him for making her tell him, for making her confront herself. "Can't you see?" she cried. "I hate being helpless and dependent! I hate being a burden! I'm clumsy and ugly...." A sob escaped her and she became still, stunned by her own outburst.

Michael understood her emotions. It was common for someone in her situation to become depressed occasionally. He'd seen it countless times. But he couldn't remember ever having a patient's distress tear at him quite so much.

"It's normal for you to feel those things," he said softly.

Dana gave a harsh laugh. "Because they're true."

"No." Michael brought his hand up, intending to wipe the moisture from her cheek. But he discovered that her pale skin was as soft as cream and he lightly caressed it instead. He wanted to say something comforting. He wanted to give her sage advice on how to deal with her depression. But the words caught in his throat. Her blue-green eyes gazed up at him and he wondered if it was possible for a man to drown on dry land just by looking at her. Her wide, full lips were parted slightly, and with a jolt he realized he wanted to kiss her.

He pulled his hand away.

It took Dana a moment to recover. When she did, heat suffused her face. Something had happened between them. She didn't know whether to welcome it or fear it.

Michael had turned away to unlock the door. "I have to go," he said. His voice was a low rasp as if it hurt him to speak. He pushed the door open wide and handed her the keys before looking at her. His gaze was guarded and unreadable. "Will you be all right?"

"Yes. Thank you." Not knowing what more to say, she turned to go inside.

"Dana?"

She stopped and looked at him. He was frowning. "What is it, Michael?"

He waited a beat, then said, "You have beautiful eyes. It's a shame to hide them."

She made no reply as he turned and walked to his car. How could she when her heart was in her throat? She went inside and closed the door.

Dana stopped in the middle of the kitchen and leaned against her walker, overwhelmed. She knew the motive behind his compliment was just a ploy to get her to leave her dark glasses at home. And yet she couldn't deny that hearing him say the words had thrilled her. It surprised her just how much.

She pressed the palm of her hand to her cheek. His touch had surprised her, as well. He'd touched her before, of course, but this time was different. This time he'd touched her as a man would touch a woman. Why?

Certainly not because of any physical attraction, she thought with self-loathing.

Maybe it was some deep-rooted need to feel wanted again, to feel attractive, that had her reading more into the gesture than had actually existed.

He'd told her to trust him. She was astonished to realize that she did—perhaps more than she trusted herself.

The door behind her flew open, startling her from her reverie. For a fraction of a second she thought Michael had returned and her heart leaped. But it was a familiar slender redhead, dressed in a tailored dark blue skirt and white blouse, who swept into the room like a restless spring breeze.

Dana smiled. "Hi, Val."

"Who was that great-looking guy pulling out of your drive?" The gold bangles on Valerie Evans's wrist clattered together as she motioned over her shoulder with a toss of her hand. Beneath the large amber frames of her prescription glasses, her ginger-tinted lips curled into a mischievous grin.

"His name is Michael Gordon. He's my physical therapist."

Valerie's tweezed brows rose under the bangs of her stylishly short hair. "I didn't know PTs made house calls." She swept past Dana, tossed her purse onto the white Formica counter and proceeded to make a pot of coffee. "Now I know why you were reluctant to talk about him the other night. You're keeping him for yourself."

Dana knew Val was teasing, but was helpless to stop the rising heat in her cheeks. She moved to the dinette and sat down, hoping to avoid her friend's scrutiny. "I needed a ride home because of a stupid mix-up on my part, and he was kind enough to offer."

Valerie tossed a glance over her shoulder. "Why didn't you tell me you needed a ride?"

"I didn't want to bother you."

Valerie flipped on the coffeemaker and turned around. Leaning with her hips against the counter, she folded her arms and said, "I told you Peter and I would share the driving."

"I know, Val, and I appreciate it. But I'm trying to regain my independence, remember?"

Her friend peered at her through her owlish glasses. "What's the real story?"

Dana sighed. "All right. I thought Steven would be free to take me."

"Where is that gorgeous brother of yours?"

"Phoenix—until tomorrow night."

"So why didn't you call me?"

"Because I know how busy you are."

Val shook her head. "That's not good enough. You know I'm more than happy to be there when you need me."

Dana's hands balled into fists on the table. "I'm tired of needing people!" she blurted.

Valerie's brows shot upward. "Now you sound like the Danny I used to know and love."

Dana stared at her, then laughed. "That's what I like about you, Val. You always know the right thing to say."

Valerie winked, then turned back to the counter and poured them each a cup of coffee, putting a generous spoonful of sugar in her own. "How's the article coming?"

"I almost have it finished," Dana replied, "but something isn't right. If you've got the time—"

"Let's take a look at what you have."

They went to the spare bedroom that Dana had converted to an office. With a computer and desk, file cabinet and drawing board crammed into the tiny room, there was barely enough space left for the two women and a walker.

Dana sat down at the computer. Val set their mugs of coffee on the desk next to her and leaned over her shoulder, using the walker as an armrest.

Flipping on the computer, Dana brought up the file she'd titled "Festival."

"Portland's biggest event of the year is about to blossom to life," the article read. "This year's Rose Festival begins with the celebration of the queen's coronation Friday at the Civic Auditorium, followed by an explosion of fireworks at Tom McCall Waterfront Park."

The article went on to list other festival events, from auto races to floral shows to concerts. Val scanned the screen, then reached over and hit the Page Up key, reading with practiced speed.

"Here," she said, stopping. "This paragraph interrupts the flow."

"You're right," Dana agreed. "What if I were to put it here?" She moved the cursor down the page.

Val nodded thoughtfully. "And this sentence needs rewording." She pointed to a line on the screen.

Twenty minutes later, they were finished. Val went to the kitchen to refill their coffee mugs, while Dana set up the printer to run off a copy.

Val returned and handed Dana one of the mugs. "So," she said, "is this Michael Gordon any good?"

Dana choked. She quickly set her coffee cup down and struggled to catch her breath.

Val thumped her a couple of times on the back, then asked, "Was it something I said?"

Dana shook her head. "I just swallowed wrong." She muttered something about checking the printer and turned away from her friend's astute gaze.

"You haven't answered my question."

Dana shrugged. "He seems okay," she commented, absently scanning the lines of print. "I've only had two sessions with him." In that short time he had managed to shred her defenses and expose her emotions with alarming ease, she mused. Why was that?

The printer finished. She tore the paper along its perforation and gathered it into a neat stack.

"I have another assignment for you," Val said.

Dana turned and handed her the printed article. "Let me guess. Fashions for the June bride? Or perhaps honeymoon retreats."

Val shot her a "get serious" look over the rim of her glasses. "Very amusing. I was thinking of something you've had firsthand experience with."

"Well that eliminates weddings and honeymoons," Dana quipped. "What did you have in mind?"

"Something on physical therapy," Val replied, "from the patient's point of view. Not just the mechanics, but how it feels. Explore the patient-therapist relationship."

Dana became very still. She'd rather not explore her relationship with Michael, friendly or otherwise. Her feelings were too unpredictable at the moment. "Do you think the timing is right for something like that?"

"Certainly. Summer's just around the corner. People will be getting out more, participating in sports and other outdoor activities, resulting in related injuries. The timing couldn't be better."

It made perfect sense. And she was the logical choice for the assignment. Then why couldn't she shake the uneasy feeling in the pit of her stomach?

"I'll start on it right away."

"Is there a problem, Danny?"

"Why do you ask?"

Valerie shrugged. "I get the feeling there's something about Mr. Gordon that you're not telling me."

Dana turned back to the computer and punched a series of keys to save the article they'd been working on and to escape the word processor. If it were only that easy to escape uncomfortable situations in real life, she thought.

"He's my PT, nothing more."

"Yes. Well, remember you said it, not me."

Before Dana could ask her what she meant by the remark, Valerie had straightened and was glancing at her sturdy gold watch. "I've got a paper to put out. Let's have lunch Saturday. You should have an outline by then."

Dana reached for her walker.

"Don't get up," Val said. "I can find my way out." She grabbed the article and tucked it under her arm. "Thanks for the coffee." She flashed Dana a broad smile. "See you Saturday."

Dana heard the kitchen door close. She was glad Val had come over. She felt productive, having turned over a finished piece to her editor. Maybe her friend was right. Maybe she *was* making progress toward becoming the Dana everyone knew before the accident—purposeful and self-reliant. She'd gotten herself to therapy today, hadn't she? Sort of. And she'd been given another assignment.

There's something about Mr. Gordon that you're not telling me. Val's comment leaped to the forefront of her thoughts.

There certainly was, Dana decided after a moment's contemplation. Her lips curled in reluctant pleasure. Michael Gordon had a captivating smile.

Chapter Five

When Michael got home he threw on a pair of running shorts and an old T-shirt and jogged across the street to Laurelhurst Park. He needed to think, and he seemed to do it best when he was on the move.

The park was one of the reasons he'd chosen to live in this particular neighborhood. The paved path around the park's circumference was nearly a mile long and ideal for running. Fingers of light filtered through the trees where the sun hung low in the sky. Once it dipped out of sight, the ornate lamps that lined the pathway would take over. Michael breathed in the fresh pine-scented air as his running shoes echoed the steady rhythm of his long, easy stride. Others occupied the path and grassy slopes—strollers, joggers, lovers—but he took little notice.

He'd dropped his guard this afternoon. Dana Whitaker had gotten to him. He couldn't allow that to happen. The fact that it had, puzzled him.

There was no denying she was beautiful. But he'd encountered beauty before. She was stubborn, smart, vulnerable—common enough qualities, although she seemed to balance those qualities better than most.

He dodged a group of young men who were laughing and punching at each other, then resumed his ground-eating pace.

It was her tears. Something about them had touched his soul. Not since Sarah had a woman been able to do that to him.

His step faltered, and he muttered a curse. Would he never forget?

Did he want to?

A patient and a reporter. Those were the two things he needed to remember if he intended to preserve his solitary, uncomplicated life. She didn't strike him as the kind of person who could probe unfeelingly into other people's lives for the sake of a story. But then he knew all too well that looks could be deceiving as the memory of another reporter—young, ambitious, and just as stubborn—surfaced from someplace deep in his mind.

I write about people.

He'd remember. He had to.

A rush of emotion hit Michael when he glanced up from the file on his desk Friday afternoon and saw the tall, lean man with black hair and unsettling eyes who accompanied Dana into the PT center.

Despite his resolve to remain unaffected, his body was tight with jealousy.

"Michael, I'd like you to meet my brother, Steven," Dana said.

The air rushed from his lungs. The resemblance was obvious. Any idiot could see it. Any idiot, that is, who wasn't allowing his emotions to control his brain.

On the heels of that thought came another. *Where the hell were you when your sister needed you?* He stood and moved toward them.

Steven stepped forward, his hand extended. "I've been wanting to meet you, to ask about my sister's progress, but I've been out of town on business."

Part of being an effective PT was the ability to read people. Michael didn't have to look very hard to see that Steven Whitaker was being honest with him. And the guy cared for his sister completely.

"It's a pleasure," he said, shaking Steven's hand.

Dana watched the exchange and wondered at the altering expressions on Michael's face. He stood an inch taller than Steven. Both were lean and strong. She hadn't realized how much she wanted the two men to like each other, until they shook hands. She couldn't explain why, but it gave her a feeling of security.

"Dana's doing well," Michael said in answer to Steven's question. "It's early yet, but she's already showing signs of improvement."

"How long before she's able to walk on her own?"

Dana looked at Michael, as anxious to hear his response as Steven was.

"That's difficult to say. A lot depends on her."

"Meaning?"

"Simply that her cooperation and attitude will play an important role in how quickly she regains full use of her leg." He tossed Dana a sidelong glance that made her cheeks warm.

Steven saw it and gave his sister a wry smile. "I understand, believe me." His gaze shifted back to Michael. "I just have one more question."

Dana held her breath and prayed it wasn't something embarrassing.

"How's the cafeteria food here?" he asked.

"Not bad," Michael said, smiling. "But don't buy coffee at the vending machine unless you've got a cast-iron stomach."

Steven chuckled. "Thanks for the warning."

After her brother left, Dana looked up to find Michael watching her. There was a crooked smile on his face.

"Just what did you do to those poor PTs at Saint Jude?"

Dana felt her cheeks flame. "Nothing that they didn't have coming," she said defensively.

"You called them incompetent."

A smile pulled at the corners of her mouth. "Among other things."

Michael laughed, loud and heartily. "I guess I should consider myself lucky."

"So far," Dana retorted, but she was no longer able to contain her smile. His laughter had that effect on her. She moved toward one of the exercise mats then, because she didn't like the way her body had begun to react to the man—like a woman in need. "Are we going to stand here and yak all day or are we going to do some exercises?'' she questioned impatiently.

''By all means.''

She had her back to him, but she heard the amusement in his voice. She decided the safest response was no response at all.

Physical therapy was exactly that—physical. There was no avoiding contact. Dana did her best to ignore the tingle that shot through her when Michael touched her bare leg, the heat of his strong hands as he assisted her labored movements. She didn't understand why it should be so difficult.

It wasn't long, though, before the exertion of the exercises caused her knee to ache until it blocked all other sensations. She clamped her teeth together and forced herself not to think about it.

''You're tensing up,'' he told her. ''Relax.''

''That's easy for you to say,'' she groaned, bringing her leg up, knee bent toward her chest.

''Quit complaining.''

Dana saw the teasing glint in his eyes. ''What do you do when you're not torturing your patients?'' she asked, lowering her leg to the mat.

''I drink blood and howl at the moon.''

She tried not to laugh at his bad joke but didn't quite succeed. ''I'm serious. Do you have any hobbies?''

''I run.'' His hands applied light pressure under her leg. ''Up,'' he ordered.

Dana brought her leg up. ''What do you mean you run?''

"I put in five or six miles a day, fifteen to twenty on weekends. I compete in hundred-mile marathons and smaller events."

Michael caught her leg before it hit the mat. "You call hundred-mile marathons a *hobby?*"

"It's how I spend my free time." His broad hands urged her leg up. "Last one," he told her.

"Why running?" she asked as she followed his instructions.

He shrugged. "It relaxes me." Her dubious expression made him smile, and he went on to explain, "It's a way to get rid of stress, or work through things that are troubling me."

Something flashed across his expression so fast that Dana dismissed it. "A physical release," she offered.

He nodded. "That, and I like the way it makes me feel—the wind against my skin, the sense of freedom."

Dana could see him racing for the sheer pleasure of it, his dark hair swept back, his muscled legs taking long, powerful strides. It would certainly be a sight worth seeing. "Why the ultramarathons?" she asked.

Michael helped her ease her leg back down to the mat before answering. "I suppose it's the challenge. I like to see how far I can push myself."

"A test of endurance."

"Right."

It made sense, she decided. Michael Gordon was the kind of man who would expect no less of himself than he did of his patients.

Then it hit her. It was the perfect angle for the article she'd been assigned to write.

She sat up and eased her legs over the edge of the mat. Michael knelt in front of her to help with her shoes. "I'd like to interview you," she stated.

His hands jerked, and he dropped the shoe. His movements were stiff and measured as he retrieved it and slipped it on her foot.

"No," he replied without looking at her.

"I think you're an interesting local personality," she continued, undaunted by his response. A lot of interviewees said no the first time. They were frightened of the idea, self-conscious, or didn't think they were interesting enough for people to want to read about them.

Michael put his hands on his knees and pushed himself to his feet. Dana was startled by the harshness in his gaze. There was tension in every muscle of his face.

"I said, no interview."

"Why?"

"Because I have a right to my privacy." He turned and walked toward his desk, his posture rigid.

Dana grabbed her walker and stood. "I can respect that, Michael. I'm not asking you to bare your soul. But there's a part of your life that I think the public would find interesting."

He stopped abruptly, turned on his heel and glared at her. "I don't give a damn what the public thinks," he growled. "Find somebody else to write about."

Dana met the anger in his eyes. It frightened her—she could hear the blood pounding in her veins, but she refused to back down. There was a reason for his violent rejection, and she intended to find out what it was.

"I can't force you to give me an interview," she said, trying a different approach. "But you have to understand, I've been given an assignment. I'll write the article with or without your help. Wouldn't you rather give your side of the story?"

"There is no story."

"There will be."

Michael's shoulders sagged, and he raked his fingers through his hair. His frown remained, but there was sadness in his eyes and in the deep grooves around his mouth. "I'm asking you not to do this, Dana."

"Are you afraid I'll write something uncomplimentary?" When he didn't answer, she went on. "You've nothing to worry about, Michael. I'm good at what I do."

"That's what I'm afraid of," he said, his voice so low Dana had to strain to hear him.

Before she could question his statement, Steven walked in. "Ready, sis?"

She glanced at her brother and nodded, then looked back at Michael. "When we first met, you told me I'd have to trust you," she said. "You could try doing the same for me."

Michael couldn't sleep. The blanket and sheet on his large bed felt like they were pinning him to the mattress. He tossed them aside and lay in his white cotton briefs, staring through the darkness at the ceiling of his room.

Sleep, dammit. Close your eyes and shut it out. He flung an arm across his eyes and lay like that for long minutes, controlling his breathing, counting each intake of stale air. There was a knot in his stomach the size of a baseball.

Swinging his legs out of bed, he went to the window and flung it open. It had rained that evening and a cool breeze brushed his bare stomach, raising tiny bumps on his skin. He leaned forward, resting the palms of his hands on the windowsill, and took long, deep breaths. He could hear the crickets and frogs singing their nightly serenade from the park across the street. The sky was a deep gray except for a muted bright spot where the moon shone. He looked closer and could see a sprinkling of stars where the cloud cover was already starting to break up. Tomorrow would be a good day for running, he thought absently.

Then he hung his head. He couldn't stop seeing the hurt in Dana's eyes. Or remembering the taste of his own fear. He could have explained it to her. He could have told her about Sarah. A shudder rippled through his body. It had been two years, but remembering was still painful. It was wrong to blame Dana for something she'd had no part in. He knew that. But a reporter's callousness had destroyed what had been left of his shattered life in L.A. and that wasn't easy to forget. Or forgive.

He straightened and closed the window. With slow, weary steps, he walked back to sit on the edge of the bed and switch on the reading light. The framed photograph on the nightstand drew his attention like a magnet. It was of a younger, more naive Michael with his arms around a tall, elegant woman. Hair the color of a summer sunset brushed her bare shoulders, and sapphire eyes looked back from a smooth classic face.

The photo had been taken on their honeymoon in Hawaii, and they were both dressed in bright flowery prints. Michael could still remember the ancient little man, a tourist himself, who had snapped the picture for them. First he'd made them laugh with his jokes. Michael would be forever grateful to him for that. It was the way he wanted to remember Sarah—laughing and carefree.

Ten short months. That was all the time he'd had with her before her death. He ran a finger along the glass over Sarah's cheek. It was cold to the touch. "I loved you," he murmured.

He switched off the light. Propping his pillows against the headboard, he sat back and pulled the covers up to his waist. Staring into the darkness once again, he saw Dana's misty blue-green eyes. She was unlike Sarah in so many ways, and yet he had a hunch she could stir feelings that were just as strong.

There had been no one in his life since Sarah. No one to laugh or cry with, or hold close in the night. No one to share his life with. He'd carefully guarded against it. He never intended to leave himself open to that kind of anguish and helplessness again.

Dana Whitaker was the last person in the world he needed to get involved with. As a patient, she was a threat to his professional reputation. As a reporter, she had the power to expose his private life and reopen old wounds.

As a woman, she challenged the wall he'd erected around his heart.

But he wanted her.

For the first time since his wife's death, he was scared.

Chapter Six

Dana couldn't bring herself to sit within the confines of her small office. Last night's rain clouds had cleared. The late-morning sun bounced prisms of color off the drops of moisture still clinging to the tips of the tree branches outside her window. A nagging restlessness had her wishing she could move faster than a snail so she could walk it off. She hadn't felt this way in so long that she didn't recognize it at first. Then she realized it was the jittery feeling she used to get when she had a big assignment to tackle—a combination of nervous anticipation, fear and excitement.

She found a spiral notepad, sharpened a new pencil, and curled up in a patch of sun on the couch.

MICHAEL GORDON, she wrote in bold letters. Since her story was about him as much as herself, it seemed like a good place to start. Maybe by jotting down what

he knew, she'd find a clue to his reason for refusing
o be written about, for his fury at the thought of it.

His chin was at eye level, which would make him a
ittle over six feet tall. "Six-one," she wrote. "Dark
rown eyes. Intense. Ruggedly handsome." She
topped, her pencil poised to strike that last part, then
lecided to leave it. The notes were for her eyes only,
ind her personal opinion might hold the key she was
ooking for.

"Athletic build. Strong. A marathon runner." She
topped again, this time in awe. In her present condi-
ion, it was a challenge just getting across the room to
inswer the phone before the caller hung up. What
lrove a man to run a hundred miles and then talk
ibout it like it was a cakewalk?

"Determined," she wrote. "Perceptive. Intimidat-
ng." Was that another personal opinion? she won-
lered.

"Faultlessly professional. Demanding. Gentle." Dr.
Stewart had been correct in saying the man was one of
he best. He hadn't backed down or tried to sugar-
coat his words when she'd challenged his ability to
telp her.

"A widower." Now there was a delicate subject. He
tadn't intended to talk about it, she was almost posi-
ive. Whatever the circumstances behind his wife's
leath, he was still suffering. He'd loved her. Dana had
he feeling Michael Gordon was capable of intense
passion. She glanced down, startled to see the words
committed to paper. She crossed them out. That was
getting a bit too personal.

"Aloof. Private." Dana snorted. That was an un
derstatement. The question was, why? Was it simply
a personal preference, or had he been driven to it?

She reread her notes. They were frustratingly brief
and insubstantial. The answer was in there some
where, but her feelings kept getting in the way. He was
a gorgeous body with deep brown eyes and a nice
smile. Nothing out of the ordinary, she told herself.

Except he was. She'd never known a man who could
stir up her emotions the way he did. He was an attrac
tive, sensitive, infuriating mystery.

She huffed and tossed the pencil and pad onto the
coffee table. Her restlessness was still there. She de
cided she may as well take advantage of her pent-up
energy and get her exercises out of the way. Grabbing
her walker, she crossed the room to the stereo unit in
front of the picture window.

As she popped in a cassette, a movement outside
caught her attention, and she looked up. Her neigh
bor, Mr. Watson, was pushing his mower out of his
garage. He glanced her way and waved. Dana smiled
and waved back. Then she looked at her own ne
glected yard and her hands tightened on her walker in
despair. Steven had mowed the lawn for her, but it was
badly in need of weeding after the long winter, and the
shrubs were getting wild-looking.

Mr. Watson's mower roared to life as the first strains
of Martha and the Vandellas spilled from the speak
ers at opposite corners of the room. Dana slid the
volume control up and moved away from the win
dow. Using her walker for support, she began to swing
her left leg in a small circular motion. She was aware

of the muscles around her knee as they stretched, then contracted—like thick elastic bands being alternately pulled and released. She shut out the pain and focused on the muscles themselves.

Quadriceps and hamstrings. The two main muscle groups of the knee. They had been explained to her in great detail, first by Dr. Stewart, then by a slew of physical therapists. She knew enough about the anatomy of the human knee to write a ten-page article on that alone, she conceded glumly.

With the continual motion came increased flexibility and her thoughts made their unerring way to Michael again. He was a pain in the backside, but she couldn't stop thinking about him with every other breath she took. There was the assignment, of course, but she had the feeling she'd think about him even if she hadn't been told to.

She'd touched a nerve yesterday. And there had been more than just anger behind his denial. Anger, she could have understood. Reporters weren't always welcomed with open arms. People liked to read the news, as long as it wasn't about them. But Michael's resentment went deeper than that. There'd been anguish in his expression.

The tempo of the music changed, and she moved to the couch to do her leg lifts.

It wasn't just his privacy he was protecting, she decided. Michael was hiding something—something that had left a painful scar. She looked down the leg she was struggling to elevate and her lip humorlessly curled. She knew about painful scars.

Suddenly the tiny hairs at the nape of her neck prickled. She caught a movement out of the corner of her eye, and a ripple of terror shot through her. She screamed and found herself looking into the startled eyes of her editor.

She clutched her hands to her heart and fell back against the couch. "Jeez, Val!" she shouted over the music. "You scared the life out of me!"

"*I* scared *you?*" Valerie shouted back. She dropped onto the couch beside Dana. "That scream of yours went right through me!"

"What are you doing sneaking up on me like that?" Dana yelled.

"I knocked, but you didn't hear me!" Valerie jabbed a bright rose fingernail at the source of the noise. "Mind if I turn that off?"

The music stopped.

A long second ticked by as both women stared at the stereo. Then the cassette deck snapped off. The unexpected sound in the sudden silence made them jump.

Dana looked at Val. "That's some power of suggestion you have."

Val held her finger up and examined it. "Must be the new nail color."

Dana laughed. "Well, don't point that thing at me."

Valerie peered at her from behind her glasses. "Judging by the way you're dressed, maybe I should. You were planning on changing, weren't you?"

Dana glanced down at her gray sweats with the stretched neckline, frayed cuffs and baggy knees, then took note of Valerie's dusty-rose blouse, black slacks and pumps, and the customary half-dozen bangles on her wrists. Not every redhead could wear that color, she silently observed, her gaze returning to the dressy blouse, but on Val it looked fabulous.

She groaned and let her head fall back against the couch. "I forgot we were having lunch today."

"That's obvious," Valerie remarked. "Mind telling me what you were thinking about when I came in?"

There was Michael again. In the short time it had taken to have the wits scared out of her, she'd forgotten him, but Val's question brought everything rushing back.

"About that assignment—"

"The one on physical therapy?"

"I need more time."

Val spotted the spiral pad on the coffee table in front of her. "Are these your notes?" she asked, leaning forward for a closer look. She had the pad in her hand before Dana could stop her.

Dana felt the heat move up her neck and into her face. "They're nothing, really," she stammered.

It took Val another second to finish reading. When she did, she tipped her head and regarded Dana with concern in her expression. "Is there something going on here that I should know about?"

Dana shot her a quick frown, ready to deny it. But meeting her friend's gaze, she found she couldn't. Instead, she sighed and muttered, "I don't know, Val. He's so...exasperating."

"And good-looking."

Dana gave a short laugh and picked at a piece of fuzz on the couch. "I've noticed."

"Maybe this assignment wasn't such a good idea."

"I want to do it," Dana admitted. Earlier in the week, she'd have done anything to get out of it, but yesterday had changed things. She had to know more about the mysterious Michael Gordon, and this assignment seemed to be the best way to do it.

She pushed her long hair behind her ear. "I've discovered that he's a runner, a supermarathoner," she explained. "He actually seems to enjoy pushing himself to the limit. I'd like to focus my story on the correlation between that and how he relates to his patients."

"Sounds great. So what's the catch?"

Dana told her what Michael had said about being interviewed.

"Then write the article without his help. You should be able to gather enough information to put a story together."

Dana wasn't as confident. It shouldn't matter to her that Michael didn't want to be written about. But it did.

"The *Gazette* will be running Rose Festival specials in the next two editions," Valerie said. "That gives you two more weeks to come up with something."

"Right." She met Valerie's gaze and forced a tiny smile. "I'm fine, really." She reached for her walker. "Give me a few minutes to change."

Val put a hand on her arm and said, "I don't want to see you get hurt, Danny. I trust your judgment, but don't rush into anything with this guy, okay? Guard your heart."

Dana remembered Michael's anger. It wasn't likely she'd be rushing into anything with him—now, or ever. The thought left her feeling strangely empty.

"Keep pedaling."

"It hurts," Dana complained solemnly from her perch on the stationary bicycle.

"Don't think about it," Michael said. "Let your body work and think about something else."

She glanced over and met his dark, perplexing gaze. His coolness toward her hurt more than the pedaling did, and she looked away. A week had passed since she'd asked him for an interview. In that time, he'd maintained careful control of his emotions. She could see it in the set of his jaw, feel it in his impersonal touch. His professionalism remained damnably admirable, his aloofness impenetrable.

She'd had her stitches removed Monday. Dr. Stewart examined her knee and was pleased with her progress. Then he'd asked her about physical therapy.

"You and your new PT getting along all right?"

"Fine," she grumbled.

To which he remarked dryly, "Your enthusiasm is certainly reassuring."

From where she lay on the examination table, Dana had to look up a long way to meet the glint of humor in her doctor's pale blue eyes. Blond, fair-skinned, even-tempered and moderately handsome, Dr. Adam Stewart was six feet three inches tall. He could have been a basketball player. Or a runner.

"How well do you know Michael Gordon?"

"We run together occasionally," he replied, confirming Dana's hunch. "Mike used to work for the PT center here."

"What made him leave?"

Dr. Stewart shrugged. "He liked the idea of working for a smaller, more community-oriented hospital. Less stress, I suppose."

"Has he ever been involved in anything illegal?" Even as she asked it, she knew it was a crazy idea. But it didn't hurt to cover all the bases.

Adam Stewart laughed. "Mike? You must be kidding. Why would you think that?"

She told him about Michael's less-than-eager attitude toward the article she had been assigned to write.

Dr. Stewart's brows dipped. "Mr. Gordon is a very private man. That doesn't make him a criminal."

Dana had to agree.

Her gaze drifted back to Michael as she continued to pedal. He wore pale gray cotton pants, an over-size gray sweatshirt with the sleeves pushed up, and white sneakers. Simple. Masculine. How she wished she could break through the barrier he'd thrown up between them. She held his gaze, determined to decipher what was behind those hooded eyes.

He frowned. "Two more minutes," he said, then turned and disappeared into an adjoining room.

Once out of sight, Michael leaned with his back against the wall and closed his eyes. "Dammit," he muttered. Every time she looked at him, he felt exposed. He was convinced that if she looked at him long enough, she'd know everything there was to know about him. She hadn't said anything more about an interview, but he wasn't optimistic enough to believe she'd dropped the idea. She was waiting for the right moment, when he had his guard down, to make her move.

In his present state, that could be any day now.

Over the past week, he'd maintained such tight control that he sometimes felt it slipping out of his grasp. And she wasn't even aware of it. If she had been, if she had intentionally attempted to charm him, he could have resisted without missing a beat. But her charm went deeper than that. It was the way she refused to give up. The way she held her head high despite the pain he knew she still endured. Her ability to find humor in her own embarrassment.

He was attracted to her despite himself. He could only hope that she continued to improve at her present rate. In another month, she'd no longer be his responsibility. She'd be out of his life.

The thought left him feeling hollow. He gave another low curse and grabbed a pair of crutches.

Dana stopped pedaling. As far as she was concerned, Michael had been gone too long. Two minutes or not, she'd had enough. She slid from the bicycle seat, putting her weight on her right leg. Pivoting, she tried to bring her left leg through the bicycle, but didn't quite clear the frame. Her hand slipped off the handlebar and she was suddenly falling backward.

"Oh, help," she muttered. Her arms flew out, but there was nothing to grab on to.

She heard something hit the carpet behind her and then Michael's arms were under hers, catching her. He hauled her against his solid frame and held her there.

"What the hell were you doing?" he growled in her ear.

She struggled against the arms wrapped around her waist and the melting sensation that threatened to take over her limbs. His warm, muscled body, molded to the length of her back, was making her brain fuzzy, and she was overcome by an urgent need to put space between them.

"I was trying to get off that contraption," she snapped. "Now, will you let me go?"

"Not until I'm sure you're all right," he snapped back. "Why didn't you wait until I could help you?"

She made a derisive sound. "And when would that have been?"

"I told you, two minutes."

Dana stopped struggling. "It seemed longer."

Michael was acutely aware of her—the fresh fragrance of her hair, her slender shoulders pressed against his chest, the way her rounded bottom curved into his groin. He could feel his body reacting to the contact, growing hard. With a groan, he put his hands on her slim waist and pushed himself away from her. She grasped the handgrip of the bicycle.

The instant he released her, her knees buckled.

"Dana—"

He grabbed her and pulled her to him again. This time they were face-to-face, with Dana's arms pinned against his chest. She looked up and Michael felt what was left of his resolve slip away, lost somewhere in the depths of her eyes. Unable to stop himself, he lowered his head, anticipating the sweetness of her soft, full lips.

From behind them came the sound of a throat being cleared and Michael brought his head up with a jerk. Steven stood to one side, watching the two of them with interest.

"We'll be a few more minutes," Michael told him.

"Take your time," Steven replied amiably.

Michael looked back at the woman crushed in his arms. Her lips were parted, her gaze fixed on his mouth. He came to the startling conclusion that she'd wanted the kiss to happen every bit as much as he had.

Even more startling was the pleasure he derived from that knowledge.

"Are you hurt?" he asked, his low voice hoarse.

"I'm fine," she murmured.

"Do you think you can grab the bicycle and keep your balance long enough for me to get your crutches?"

"Crutches?" There was a flicker of hope in her blue-green eyes when they met his gaze.

Michael couldn't help but smile. "You're ready."

"Hey, sis, that's great!"

Dana gave an uneasy laugh and glanced over at her brother. "Let's see how I do on them before we get too excited, shall we?"

Moments later, she was circling the room with a crutch tucked under each arm. She'd been instructed in how to use crutches before, so Michael had little to do but watch and share in her exhilaration. She was smiling broadly when she came to a stop beside her brother.

He put his arm across her shoulders and gave her a squeeze that threatened to pull her off-balance. "This is a good sign, right?" he asked, looking at Michael.

Michael tore his gaze away from Dana's smile. "Yes. She's made a lot of progress in the last two weeks."

For the first time since having had her stitches removed, Dana allowed herself to feel happy. It could have been Steven's infectious enthusiasm, but she would be lying to herself if she didn't admit that hearing Michael's praise had something to do with it, as well.

"This calls for a celebration," Steven declared. "I'd like to take you and sis out to dinner tomorrow night."

Dana's heart stopped, then raced. She glanced over at Michael to see how he was taking the sudden invitation. He looked terrified.

Understandable. She had some misgivings of her own. Common sense told her to be thankful that Steven had come in when he did, but the woman in her wanted to strangle him. Could she trust herself to have dinner with the man and not make a fool of herself?

On the other hand, it was the perfect opportunity to get some information out of him for her story. "I think that's a wonderful idea," she offered.

"It'll give you a chance to meet Beverly," Steven continued.

Dana forgot Michael for a moment and looked up at her brother. "Beverly?"

"A new friend of mine," he explained with a smile. "She moved into the apartment next to mine last weekend." He gave Dana's shoulders another squeeze, then looked back at Michael. "So what do you say?"

"I appreciate the invitation," Michael said, "but I wouldn't want to intrude."

"You'd hardly be intruding. You're the reason sis is doing so well. It wouldn't be a celebration without you."

Michael barely acknowledged the compliment. He was watching Dana. He wished to God he knew what she was thinking. Not that it would have made any difference. As insane as it sounded, he wanted to accept Steven's invitation. Like a kid with a book of matches, he knew he shouldn't, but the temptation was too great. He wanted the opportunity to see Dana as a woman rather than a patient. His chest began to ache, and he realized he was holding his breath.

She smiled then, and the air rushed from him. "Yes, Michael, please join us."

Michael shifted his gaze to Steven. "It would be my pleasure."

Chapter Seven

"Look out!"

At Adam's shout, Michael saw the poodle sniffing the shrubs by the path's edge in time to leap over it, narrowly missing the startled animal. Muttering an oath, he fell back into step beside his running partner.

Since his transfer from Saint Jude, Michael's runs were usually solitary, but today Dr. Adam Stewart kept pace next to him, his fair skin and thinning flaxen hair a contrast to Michael's darker, tanned coloring. Adam stood two inches taller, but weighed almost twenty pounds less, his lean frame less muscled. Michael was the stronger runner, but Adam's longer legs easily kept pace.

Michael generally avoided the park on Saturday afternoons. Too many people. And dogs. But Adam had come by, and they couldn't pass up the chance to run together. And Michael had thought a good run was just what he needed to clear his head.

So far, it wasn't working.

"That was close," Adam remarked, his words coming out in short bursts.

"Yeah."

"Mind telling me what's up?"

He was a damn fool, that's what. He'd tried convincing himself that there was nothing wrong with having dinner with Dana. After all, her brother and his date would be there.

Date. That was the clincher. The whole thing sounded more like a double date than a harmless celebration.

"If you don't want to talk to me," Adam drawled, "just say so."

Michael glanced over at the wry expression on his friend's face. "Sorry, Ad. I've got a lot on my mind."

"No kidding."

They switched onto another path and a neon yellow Frisbee bounced off Michael's chest. He barely avoided colliding with the young boy who was chasing after it.

"Sorry!" the boy shouted.

Michael waved and kept running. He hadn't gotten very far when he realized Adam was no longer beside him. He stopped and turned. His doctor friend was a few yards back, doubled over with his hands on his knees, laughing.

Michael jogged back toward him. "What the hell's gotten into you?" he asked, although he had a pretty good idea. They were standing in almost the very spot where he'd encountered the Frisbee.

Adam straightened, looked at him, and started laughing again.

"It wasn't that funny," Michael grumbled, but he couldn't stop the corners of his mouth from twitching. It *was* funny, dammit. Dana was muddling his brain, and his body was following suit.

Another pair of runners was headed in their direction. Michael and Adam moved to a grassy spot at the path's edge and sat down.

"Oh, God," Adam gasped, wiping at his eyes with the bottom of his sweatshirt, "I haven't laughed that hard in ages."

"Glad I could oblige." Michael's remark was dry as he stretched his legs out in front of him and leaned back on his elbows.

Adam propped himself up with one arm, resting the other on his raised knee, and regarded him. "Are you going to tell me the cause of this clumsiness?"

Michael studied the toes of his running shoes. "It's that problem patient you sent me."

"Dana Whitaker?"

He gave a reluctant nod. He wasn't sure he wanted to talk about it—even to his closest friend.

"Don't tell me she's been giving you a hard time, too?"

"Not in the way you think," Michael grumbled.

There was silence. He looked over and saw Adam studying him with a sly smirk on his face.

"What're you smiling about?" he questioned testily.

"You're attracted to her."

"The hell I am," he lied. He looked down the length of his legs to the toes of his running shoes again. He didn't like lying to his friend. He sighed and muttered, "At least, I shouldn't be."

"Why not?"

He met Adam's gaze with a frown. "Because she's a patient, that's why." It was the truth. A fraction of it, anyway. He wasn't ready to go into the other reasons at the moment. If ever.

"How does she feel about you?" Adam asked.

"I don't know." That wasn't the complete truth, either. Michael was aware that Dana had been ready to let him kiss her, but he wasn't sure why. Was it him she was interested in, or the story she thought she could get? Was dinner tonight merely an opportunity for her to squeeze information out of him?

He shot Adam a sidelong glance. "Let's drop it, okay?" But it wasn't a question.

"Does this have anything to do with the interview she wants?" his friend pressed.

Michael met his gaze squarely. "You know about that?"

"She asked me if you might be hiding something illegal."

Michael's short laugh was harsh. "What did you tell her?"

Adam shrugged. "Only that being a private man doesn't make you a criminal."

No, Michael thought, it didn't. Unfortunately, not everyone believed it. He looked at his friend. Adam didn't know about Sarah or his reasons for leaving a high-paying position at Los Angeles General Hospital. He'd answered out of trust. "Thanks, Ad. I appreciate it."

Adam grinned. "What're friends for?" He leaned back on his elbows and looked up at the sky. "So what're you going to do about her?"

"I'm going to have dinner with her tonight."

The sun's afternoon rays slanted through the living room window across Dana's sketch pad and easel, warming the left side of her body. She had Tchaikovsky's "Serenade for Strings" on the stereo. The charcoal pencil felt foreign in her hand. Since her job with the *Gazette,* she'd had little time for sketching. But she'd needed something to take her mind off the fact that in two hours she would be having dinner with Michael.

As a child she had spent hours watching her mother paint beautiful landscapes. At the age of six, she was given her first easel and set of paints, which she attacked enthusiastically, trying to make her small, uncoordinated hands create the same beauty.

Over the years, she came to the conclusion that she would never be a good painter. Her landscapes were mediocre, at best. Not willing to give up on the arts altogether, she began to experiment with other mediums, and discovered she was reasonably adept at sketching the human figure. Her sharp memory was not only a valuable asset to her journalism, but she could visualize faces as well, transferring them from her mind onto paper, capturing a person's essence—a fleeting expression, the curve of a cheek—as she now tried to do with her father's image.

Gradually, her movements became more fluid, the charcoal an extension of her hand and mind, as she sketched the familiar, loving lines of his face, the wisdom of age, his gentleness. After a time, she sat back and studied her work. Her father smiled at her with a barely perceptible twinkle in his eyes. She was pleased with the results.

Flipping to a clean page in her sketch pad, she began outlining another face from memory. It was a bold, yet kind face, with strong distinctive features—a broad brow, straight nose and square chin. His penetrating dark eyes held a hint of mystery and reserve. One corner of his mustache was slightly higher than the other in a half smile, with only his lower lip showing. Dana ran the tip of her little finger lightly over the lip line to soften it, caress it. Her sun-warmed body grew warmer as she remembered how intensely she had wanted him to kiss her yesterday.

He was arrogant, strong-willed, and yet intuitive, compassionate. A confusing contradiction. His gaze could be gentle and understanding one instant, cold and aloof the next. His broad hands tortured her body with their exercises, but she'd felt their tenderness also.

As she stared into the dark eyes she had sketched, Musetta's waltz from *La Bohème* began to play. Michael gazed back at her from the page and an odd sensation came over her, as if the man and the music were connected in some way. The longer she stared at the sketch, mesmerized, the more she was drawn into a feeling of relativity that she couldn't quite grasp.

The waltz was one of her favorites. She had fallen in love with it the first time she'd heard it on a Public Broadcasting program. She could almost imagine gliding across a ballroom floor with Michael to the lilting orchestration, their bodies pressed together in sensual rhythm.

The music stopped and the image slipped away. But the sensation of a tenuous bond between man and music remained, and she puzzled over it. There was often soft background music playing at the PT center. Could she have heard it there and unconsciously associated it with Michael?

No. As much as she enjoyed the melody, she would have remembered hearing it. It was a case of frazzled nerves. That was all.

She peered around the sketch pad to the clock on the VCR and cursed her brother when she saw what time it was. "You and your bright ideas," she mumbled, slapping the charcoal pencil into its tray.

It took her over an hour to decide what to wear. She finally settled on a white cotton sundress with lace accents. The loose-fitting bodice, held up by thin shoulder straps, was gathered at the waist, then flared into a full, midcalf-length skirt that covered the scar on her knee. A thin chain circled her delicate neck, a strand of gold against her ivory skin. She pulled her hair away from her face with pearl combs, letting it hang loose down her back, and allowed herself a few precious seconds to gaze wistfully at the white slingbacks on the shoe rack—so similar to the ones Marla had been wearing, she realized gloomily—before slipping a pair of flat-soled sandals onto her nylon-clad feet. She was far from pleased with the pale, fragile woman who stared back at her critically from the full-length mirror.

She made her way to the bathroom to take care of her makeup. A light foundation and brush-on blush. Her hand shook as she applied mascara to her lashes. Her dinner companions were due to arrive at any moment.

She was almost finished when the doorbell rang, making her flinch and smear black goo on her eyelid.

"Darn it," she muttered, wiping at it frantically. The smudge spread and the doorbell sounded again.

"Come in!" she yelled.

She heard the door open. "Dana?"

Michael! Her heart somersaulted in her chest. "I'll just be a minute!" She looked at her reflection in the bathroom mirror and groaned.

Michael stepped inside and closed the door. Pushing his hands into the pockets of his cotton slacks, he surveyed his surroundings. The room was small, but bright. Off-white walls, sculptured desert tan carpeting, a couch and recliner in varied shades of green. Functional and neat. A reflection of the woman who lived there.

She liked music, he noted, seeing the collection of albums and cassettes under the stereo. There were a few framed photos over the television. He recognized Dana and her brother in a couple of them. An oil painting of a stormy beach, done in deep pinks and vivid blues, hung on the wall behind the couch.

As his gaze came full circle, he saw the easel and pad in front of the window and moved closer. The sketch was of an older man with features that were somehow familiar. Michael glanced at the photos over the television again and saw the same face there. Her father. Looking back at the sketch, he was struck by the artist's sensitive rendition.

Curious, he lifted the page to see if there were other sketches, and found an image of himself staring back at him. It was him, and yet there was something about the expression that was different. The eyes looked almost haunted, and there was a softness to his mouth that he'd never noticed when he looked in the mirror.

Dana watched him from the doorway. He was dressed in pleated navy slacks and a loose-fitting white dress shirt. His dark brown hair was combed away from his face and curled over his shirt collar, his expression thoughtful as he studied her sketch of him. His sheer masculinity dominated the small room.

Sensing her presence, he turned. The look of approval in his gaze as it traveled the length of her made her already-erratic heart pound rapidly. So much for cool and unaffected, she thought.

"Hello," he said, smiling.

"Hi." When had her voice become breathy? she wondered. She moved into the room and tried again, "I'm glad you could make it."

"Thank you. So am I." More than he'd anticipated, he realized. It was the first time he'd seen her in something other than sweats and shorts. He wasn't disappointed. She looked enticingly feminine in white, the crutches giving her an air of vulnerability. He saw the color in her cheeks deepen under his admiring gaze and felt a brief surge of male pride.

He turned away from her and the course of his thoughts. "Are these your work?" he asked, indicating the sketches.

"My hobby," she corrected, then shrugged. "It helps me relax."

"And you do them from memory?"

"I enjoy drawing on the impressions people make in my mind, rather than having a model to look at."

He glanced at the sketch of himself again and felt exposed. She'd discovered a part of him he'd kept hidden even from himself. The woman was talented as well as beautiful. A dangerous combination.

"I'm impressed," he admitted.

"Thank you. I'm afraid I'm a little rusty. This is the first time I've done any sketching in months."

"Have you ever sold any of your work?"

"No," she said, laughing at the thought. "My mother is the artist in the family." She glanced over at the seascape that had been a housewarming gift.

"She's very talented," Michael acknowledged.

"She has some of her work on display in a small gallery in Seaside."

"With your talent, I'm surprised you didn't follow in her footsteps."

Dana gave him a bemused smile as she crossed the room to close the drapes. "I'm a realist who likes to eat," she said. "Mom has someone to support her if her work doesn't sell. I don't." She reached for the drapery cord, and one of her crutches fell to the carpet.

Michael pulled his hands from his pockets and came toward her. "Let me help you with that." He picked up the crutch and handed it back to her, then stepped behind her to close the drapes.

Dana felt the heat of his body even though he hadn't touched her. The alluring scent of his musky aftershave clouded her thoughts and she moved away.

"What made you decide to be a journalist?"

It wasn't so much the question as the tone in which it was asked that alerted Dana's senses. She remembered his silence that day in the car when she'd told him about her work. She remembered his angry refusal to be interviewed. When she turned to look at him, his face was cast in shadow and gave no clue to his thoughts.

"It's interesting work," she answered, choosing her words carefully. "I enjoy the challenge of searching for facts and writing a story that will attract readers. I get to meet all sorts of people, and I'm always learning something new."

As she spoke, she made her way to the table at the end of the couch and switched on the tall ceramic lamp. The tenseness in Michael's expression was thrown into harsh relief.

Dana regarded him with a frown, her hands tight on her crutches. "Is it me you object to?" she asked determinedly. "Or is it journalism in general that you detest?" He turned away from her. She heard his heavy sigh and half expected him not to answer.

"It's something that happened a long time ago," he said, his voice low and expressionless. "It has nothing to do with you."

She would have liked to believe that. "Maybe you'll tell me about it sometime," she softly offered.

Michael felt a hot rush of resentment shoot through him. *Don't hold your breath, beautiful!* Then he turned and looked at her.

Yes. She was beautiful. And a whole lot more. The blue-green eyes that returned his gaze were full of caring, the curve of her mouth gentle. *Damn.* The one thing he'd focused his anger and pain on after Sarah's death stood before him in a beautiful, tender package, open and trusting, wanting to understand.

Dana saw his conflicting emotions—the anger that contorted his handsome face and sent a chill through her, and the uncertainty and longing in his dark chocolate eyes. It wasn't Dana, the journalist, but Dana, the woman, who ached to know what it was that seemed to be tearing him up inside.

The telephone on the end table next to her shrilled through the heavy silence. She glared at the offensive instrument and considered not answering it. She glanced back at Michael, but he had already turned away.

Muttering a silent oath, she answered the phone with a terse, "Hello?"

"Hi, sis."

"Steven? Where are you?"

"Home. Bev cancelled out on me at the last minute. You and Michael go on without us. He showed, didn't he?"

"Yes, but—"

"Great! The reservation is under Gordon at the Acapulco. If you can cover the check, I'll pay you back," he explained. "Will that be a problem?"

"No, but—"

"Good. Have a nice evening. Bye!"

Dana stood with the receiver buzzing in her ear and feeling like she'd just been thrown from a merry-go-round.

"Is anything wrong?"

Michael had moved closer and was watching her. She placed the receiver in its cradle. "Steven and Beverly won't be coming."

"Nothing serious, I hope."

"No." *Unless you take into account what I'm going to do to my scheming brother when I get my hands on him!* "It seems Beverly has made other plans," she said with forced calm.

"Where does that leave us?"

Us. She swallowed hard. So much for calm. "The reservation has been made," she said. "We could still go to dinner. That is, if you want to."

"Yes, I do."

The deep timber of his voice rippled through her. Good grief, how could he make three little words sound so sensuous? She had no idea what condition her nerves would be in when the evening was over, but she knew there was no way she was going to let it end here.

She gave a tentative smile. "I'll get my sweater."

* * *

The Acapulco was bustling—common for the popular restaurant on a Saturday night. The mellow strains of guitar music were barely audible over the steady drone of conversation in the crowded foyer. Conscious of her ungainliness, Dana headed for a place as close to the wall as possible, out of the way of people's toes. Michael followed, his light touch at the small of her back as intimate as it was reassuring.

"I'll go check on the reservation," he said, bringing his mouth close to her ear.

She knew he did it so she could hear him better, but that didn't stop a tingle from shooting through her at the brush of his breath on her skin. She turned to make a reply and found herself staring at his mustache. Her gaze flicked upward only to discover his dark brown eyes were just as unnerving.

"It's under Gordon," she told him, her voice a bit husky.

Michael's brow lifted. "Was that Steven's idea or yours?"

Dana gave a short laugh despite her irritation with her brother. "Steven made the reservation."

Michael gave her a crooked, knowing smile. Amazing, Dana thought, steadying herself with her crutches, how a simple muscle contraction like a smile could make her feel so weak.

"I'll be right back," he promised.

Dana hadn't realized how much courage she drew from his presence until she lost sight of him in the crowd. She felt vulnerable, afraid someone would trip over her crutches, or back into her, or she would lose her footing on the uneven ceramic-tiled floor.

Long minutes later, he reappeared at her side and placed his broad, warm hand at the small of her back once again. "Our table will be ready in a few minutes." He paused and searched her face. "How are you feeling?"

"A little skittish," she admitted with a nervous laugh. "I'm not much on crowds lately."

"I thought so." Michael positioned himself between her and the main flow of traffic, his chest a wall of security. "Better?"

Dana nodded. It was silly, she knew—an unfair burden to put on his shoulders—but she felt that nothing would happen to her as long as he was with her.

She was aware only of him—the warmth of his body, his strength, his smell, musky and clean—the occasional brush of her bare arm across the front of his shirt sending tiny electric charges through her. She tried to remind herself that she was here to get information, but she couldn't ignore the fact that her dinner companion was the most attractive, intriguing man she'd ever had the pleasure of going out with.

She glanced up at him once. He was looking out across the dining room as if deep in thought. She would get into those thoughts somehow, she vowed.

Michael's name was called, and a young, dark-haired hostess, dressed in a bright print skirt and white blouse, showed them to a booth. "Your waiter will be with you in a moment," she said, handing them each a menu.

The restaurant, with its pleasant 'south-of-the-border' atmosphere, was decorated in earth-tone tiles and heavy dark wood. A bright mosaic over the arched entry added a splash of color to the white stucco walls. Cool greenery in woven baskets hung from the beamed ceiling. The booths, with short curtains between them for privacy, lined two outer walls.

"This is nice," Michael commented. "Do you come here often?"

Dana smiled, more relaxed now that she was seated and out of the crush. "Steven brought me here for my birthday a few years ago. We don't get out together very often, but when we do we always seem to end up here. I think there must be some Mexican in our bloodline that we don't know about."

Michael was enchanted. By her story. By her smile. He watched her open her menu and study it, barely recognizing her as the bitter young woman who had stormed into the PT center, and his life, two weeks ago. His gaze went to the thick raven hair that fell across her shoulders, a sharp contrast to her creamy skin. Yes, he could picture her locked away in some remote Spanish hacienda by a doting father, bent on protecting her from rogues, like himself, who would have their way with her. He imagined what it would be like to bury his face in that hair.

"See anything you like?" she asked, looking up. Comprehension flashed in her eyes when she saw the closed menu in his hands and the intent way he was looking at her. Her cheeks flamed, but Michael was the first to look away. He opened his menu and fixed his gaze on the print, silently berating himself. He had come tonight with a purpose—to catch Dana at her own game. She could ask her questions, if that was her intention, and he would tell her no more than he wanted her to know. In the process, he would ask some questions of his own and see how she liked it.

Instead, he was caught staring at her like some lovesick adolescent.

"Good evening." A young man wearing a bold shirt and black slacks appeared at their table. He placed a basket of tortilla chips and a small bowl of salsa between them. "Are you ready to order?"

Michael closed his unread menu and looked at Dana. "Since you've eaten here before, why don't you order for both of us?"

She smiled and closed her menu. "We'll both have the Fiesta Grande."

"Good. May I get you something from the cantina while you wait?"

"I'd like a strawberry margarita," she replied.

Michael ordered a dark beer. After the waiter collected the menus and left, he leaned forward and asked, "What is a Fiesta Grande?"

A teasing light twinkled in Dana's eyes. "A surprise." She enjoyed having the advantage over him for a change, even if it was something as simple as a Mexican salad.

His low chuckle vibrated through her like the deep resonant chords of a cello being strummed. He was making mincemeat of her nervous system with his charm and casual good looks. She felt like a teenager on her first date—awkward and tongue-tied, yet pretty and desired. She was wasting precious time letting herself feel like a woman instead of thinking like a reporter. But darn it, she hadn't felt like a woman in so very long.

She took a tortilla chip and swirled it in the dish of salsa. "How long have you been a physical therapist, Michael?" She raised the chip to her mouth and caught his gaze. She'd been afraid he would resent the question. The amusement in his expression took her by surprise.

"About twelve years," he answered.

Maybe this wasn't going to be as difficult as she'd expected, Dana dared to hope, at the same time wondering at his change in attitude. "Did you go to school here in Portland?" she asked.

"No."

She waited for him to elaborate. Instead, he helped himself to a chip.

Dana decided to try another tactic. "Where did you work before Saint Jude?"

"Out of state," he replied. "Does Steven do this sort of thing often?"

Dana blinked. "Pardon me?"

Michael met her startled gaze, his own frustratingly calm. "It's obvious we were set up. I was curious to know whether your brother is in the habit of playing matchmaker."

"No. That is, I'm usually too busy to go along with his schemes."

"But he does think you don't get out enough."

Dana studied him. "Something like that," she answered slowly.

Their drinks arrived. Dana stirred her margarita with the tiny straw, then lifted it to her lips and took a sip. The icy, berry-flavored drink slid down her throat, sending a brief sharp pang to her temples. She hadn't eaten since the breakfast she'd picked at hours ago. With the second sip, she felt the tequila's warmth spread through her.

Michael poured beer into a frosted mug. "Are you disappointed he isn't here?"

"No." She looked at him when she said it. She wanted him to know...what? That she'd wanted to be alone with him?

She was tempted to ask him the same thing but was afraid to. She wasn't sure enough of herself yet, or why he was here with her. She wasn't sure she could take his answer if it turned out to be something she didn't want to hear.

"Frankly, I'm never anxious to meet Steven's latest love interest," she admitted.

"You don't approve of his choice in women?"

"I keep hoping that someday he'll be attracted to a woman for her brains instead of her physical endowment."

Michael smiled, but his gaze was thoughtful. "Don't you think it's possible for a woman to have both brains and beauty?" he asked, his deep voice soft. He leaned forward and rested his elbows on the table, bringing his presence closer. "Maybe he's having trouble finding someone like his sister."

Dana felt her heart lurch into overdrive, heard it pounding in her ears, as the room and everything in it, except Michael's captivating eyes, faded into oblivion. There was nothing lewd or suggestive in the way he looked at her, and yet she felt as if she'd just been thoroughly seduced.

Damn him! He was doing it on purpose to sidetrack her. She took another sip of her drink and set the glass down. "What about you? Are you sorry Steven and Beverly aren't here?"

"No."

If possible, his eyes had gotten darker and his low voice, as intent as his gaze. Dana couldn't think of a thing to say.

The arrival of their waiter rescued her from her dilemma. He served them each a plate with a huge tortilla shell that had been deep fried into the shape of a tall, fluted bowl, filled with refried beans, bits of chicken breast, tomato and shredded lettuce, and topped with guacamole and sour cream.

"Is there anything else I can get for you?" he asked.

Michael glanced at Dana. She shook her head. "No, thank you," he told the waiter.

"Enjoy your meal."

Michael eyed his dinner with a raised brow.

"Maybe you would have preferred something else?" Dana asked.

"No, this is fine." He shot her a crooked smile. "How do you eat it?"

She laughed, then showed him how. She broke off a piece of the shell, dipped it in the guacamole and sour cream, and popped it into her mouth.

Michael gave it a try and the side of his tortilla "bowl" crumbled onto his plate.

Dana covered her mouth with her napkin, but Michael saw the merriment in her eyes and chuckled. "I guess it takes a gentler touch."

She wiped at her mouth and laid her napkin back on her lap. "I'm sorry," she said, trying hard to contain her laughter, "I should have warned you."

"Don't apologize. I'm enjoying myself." More than you realize, he mused. He'd learned she could be flustered by him and that pleased him beyond words—possibly because he knew she had the ability to do the same to him. Then again, it could have been something deeper. Something he would store away and think about later.

He gathered some of the smaller pieces of fried tortilla and sprinkled them over his salad. "It's not every day I get to play with my food," he remarked, smiling. He picked up his fork to sample his masterpiece.

Again Dana laughed. His sense of humor was putting her at such ease that she was able to enjoy the meal in spite of her annoying habit of forgetting why she was there. As they ate, her mind came back to something he'd said earlier and it started her wondering.

"Do you have any brothers or sisters, Michael?"

He swallowed and answered, "No, I'm an only child." His smile was rueful. "And spoiled rotten."

"Really? I find that hard to believe. You give so much of yourself to your patients—"

"Not what you'd expect of a brat?" he interrupted with a teasing look in his eyes.

She smiled. "I guess not."

He looked down at his plate and pushed the remainder of his salad around with his fork. "Life has a way of humbling even the worst of brats." A pensive expression tugged at his features. He set his fork down and met her gaze. "I envy you and your relationship with your brother. I missed that when I was growing up."

"What about your parents?"

"Dad passed away five years ago. He spent a lot of time away from home, on business, so he and I never got to know each other very well." Then a tender smile crossed his face. "Mom loved me no matter how bad I was. She lives in Denver with her sister."

"Is that where you're from?"

He took a drink of beer and wiped his mustache with his napkin. *Careful.* He tried to shut out the memories that her question stirred in the back of his mind. "I moved up here from Los Angeles," he told her.

"What made you leave all that sunshine for Portland?"

It came back to him as clearly as if it had happened yesterday—the pain, the anger, the humiliation. He was standing at the end of a long, polished table, surrounded by members of the hospital's administration.

"You understand, this is no reflection on your work," a stern-faced man with graying hair told him, "and I can assure you that you'll receive an outstanding letter of recommendation. But in light of recent events, we feel it would be best if you transferred to

another hospital. Los Angeles General doesn't need your kind of publicity.''

"Michael?" He looked at her, but it was as if he were in some distant place. There was sorrow in his gaze, yet his mouth was a grim slash. Dana tried again, asking softly, "Why did you leave L.A.?"

Long seconds later, he answered, "There was no reason to stay after Sarah died."

"Sarah, your wife?"

He nodded.

"I'm sorry. It must have been very hard on you. If you ever need someone to talk to..."

The sudden contempt in his eyes froze the rest of the sentence in her throat. She saw his hand tighten around his beer mug.

"It'll be a cold day in hell before I talk to a reporter," he said.

Chapter Eight

Michael's harsh words drove the color from her face. Her heart constricted, his insult like a clamp on the vulnerable organ. Then just as quickly, the clamp released, and blood suffused her features in hot anger.

She set her empty glass down hard and grabbed her purse. Pulling some bills from her wallet, she tossed them onto the table. "This should cover the meal," she said, barely controlling the rage that shook her voice.

Michael captured her hand. "Dana, wait."

She jerked her arm and he released her without a struggle. "I'm going home," she told him. She slung her purse strap over her shoulder and grabbed her crutches.

"Dammit, I didn't mean it!"

She stopped and met his gaze with a cold look. "Yes, you did. I don't know what your problem is, but I'm not about to sit here and let you talk to me that way."

She wrestled her crutches out of the booth and stood. Michael came around the table and blocked her path.

Dana glared at the top button of his shirt. "You're bigger, and you're stronger than I am," she said through clenched teeth, "but if you don't get out of my way, I'll scream."

"Please don't."

His softly spoken plea drew her gaze upward. The look of distress in his eyes was nearly her undoing. She took a deep breath to steady her nerves. Why did he have to be standing so close? And why did he have to be so darned appealing?

"I'd like the chance to apologize," he said, "and to explain. Is there someplace where we can talk?"

She swallowed hard and reminded herself that she was furious with him. "You can take me home," she told him abruptly. "We can talk there." She wasn't at all certain that it was a wise choice, but at least there she could have the satisfaction of tossing him out if he gave her cause.

"I'd prefer someplace more neutral."

It wasn't a command, but a request. Dana felt herself giving in.

"I know a place by the river," she finally said.

On any given day during the summer, the M. James Gleason boat-landing on the Columbia River was the scene of constant activity. People came in droves to launch their boats, or bring them in. Others came just to watch, or play in the sand at the river's edge. But it was early in the season yet. The water was cold and high from the spring runoff, and the evenings brisk. Michael and Dana had the spot to themselves.

Michael stood on the bank overlooking the boat ramp, his hands thrust in his pockets, and gazed at the lights on the opposite shore almost a mile away. Below him, he could hear the rhythmic lap of water against the dock where it extended out into the river.

Dana sat on a wooden bench a few feet behind him. Other than to give directions to the boat landing, she hadn't spoken to him. Michael knew he owed her an explanation, but he didn't know where to start. Or how much to tell her. He wanted her to understand why he'd reacted the way he had, but he'd never talked to anyone about Sarah before—at least not about her death.

Without turning, he said, "Sarah was a cardiologist at L.A. General. I was the director of the hospital's physical therapy center. I'd only been working there a short time when we met." He stopped and smiled to himself, remembering the day he'd marched up to Cardiology to give the hotshot doctor a piece of his mind over the scheduling of a patient. He'd heard about Sarah Wentworth—that she was the best surgeon the hospital had, with a temper to match. That hadn't stopped him.

But nobody had prepared him for the tall, elegant woman he found himself face-to-face with. Instead of discussing his patient, he'd asked her out to dinner. Two months later they were married.

"She was so radiant and full of energy," he continued. Just as remembering could bring a smile to his face, it also pulled at an old wound that had yet to heal, and his smile became a thin line. "I didn't find out until months later that her energy came from a bottle of pills. She was addicted to amphetamines."

"Oh, Michael..."

He turned at the sound of Dana's voice. He'd almost forgotten she was there. *Why* she was there. He walked over and sat next to her, avoiding the sympathy in her eyes.

"I don't know how long she'd been using. She was very good at hiding it. On the few occasions that I caught her taking pills she always seemed to have a legitimate excuse."

The low whine of jet engines from the airport down the road filled the silence. The sound grew to a roar as the commercial plane took off, flying low over them. Michael watched it and wished he were on it.

When the plane was just a small point of light in the sky, he went on. "One night, while I was...out," he said, his tongue stumbling over the word, "her heart stopped. She was dead by the time I got home." Hunching forward, he leaned his elbows on his knees and put his head in his hands, fighting back the memory of Sarah's lifeless body, his gut-wrenching wail of denial and the overwhelming helplessness of that night.

He jumped when Dana touched his shoulder.

"I'm sorry," she murmured.

He wasn't able to look at her as he sat up and leaned against the back of the bench. He knew what he'd see in her expression.

Her hand still rested on his shoulder. He could feel her warmth reach inside him. He had the crazy urge to lay his head in her lap and let her comfort him. But he didn't. He didn't deserve her compassion.

"Somehow the local paper got wind of it," he said, his voice a harsh whisper. "They ran a story about drug abuse among surgeons and used Sarah as an example. Her life was put on display. She was dead, and all they could think about was their precious newspaper."

Dana felt him shudder. It went through her fingers, straight to her heart. Insensitive, selfish, she labeled the reporters...and a lump lodged in her throat as she thought of all the times she'd come close to doing the same thing. There was a fine line between reporting the news and invading a person's privacy.

"I refused to be interviewed," Michael continued, his words stinging. "But there was one reporter who wouldn't take no for an answer. He was convinced that I was hiding something. He'd sit outside my house. He'd follow me to work and be waiting in the parking lot. He dogged me day and night, like a vulture, determined to find some personal scrap of information to write about."

Dana swallowed. "What did you do?"

"I called the police, but he hadn't broken the law. He had the freedom of the press behind him. There was nothing I could do to stop it." Michael shrugged abruptly, with finality. "I guess he lost interest after a while, because I stopped seeing him around. In the meantime, I was politely asked to quit my job."

"That's when you moved to Portland?"

"I couldn't stand the sight of Los Angeles anymore."

Dana squeezed her eyes shut for a moment against the tears his answer aroused. "I don't know what to say, Michael. It shouldn't have happened. Sometimes a reporter oversteps the bounds of good judgment in trying to find the one story that will open the door to his career." Her defense sounded hollow even to her.

"I had a right to grieve for the loss of my wife in private." The anger in his eyes when he turned and looked at her made her flinch. "What about all the good she did for people?" he demanded. "The lives she saved? Nothing was said about that. She made one stupid mistake..."

An expression of raw pain etched his face and he looked away.

"One stupid mistake," he repeated roughly.

His mistake, not hers. And she was dead because of it.

He looked at the woman sitting next to him. There were tears in her eyes, and a pang of remorse twisted inside him. "It wasn't you, Dana. The things you asked triggered memories I didn't want to think about. That didn't give me the right to talk to you the way I did. I'm sorry."

"I accept your apology."

"You're still going to write the story, aren't you?"

"It's my job."

He sighed, not with regret, but in acknowledgement. "I won't try to stop you, but I hope you understand why I can't cooperate."

"I understand." But it still hurt. "Not all journalists are insensitive to other people's feelings," she said quietly.

As before, he brought his hand up to wipe a tear from her face. He touched first one cheek, then the other, slowly, deliberately. Dana sucked in a breath and held it. "I'm finding that out," he murmured. His words were as soft as the fingers he pushed through her hair. They lingered there for several heartbeats, then he leaned closer and brushed his lips across hers.

Dana hadn't realized that a touch could have such power. His mouth closed over hers, and she felt as if the bench had been pulled out from under her. She gripped his shoulders against the dizziness that swept over her. His lips were warm and firm and edged with a hunger she could identify with. Yet, for such a strong man, his touch was incredibly gentle.

Her lips parted with a sigh and his tongue met hers. She liked the way he tasted and the rough caress of his mustache on her face. An overwhelming need swelled inside her, nameless and potent. Sensuality? Loneliness? She didn't think about the fact that he was her physical therapist. For the moment, he was simply a man. A healer of another kind.

He made a sound deep in his throat and pulled away. Dana met his dark gaze, her mind reeling from the intensity of the feelings that surged through her, and saw the torment in his eyes.

"I shouldn't have done that," he groaned.

"I think it took us both by surprise," she acknowledged, her voice a breathy whisper.

"Surprise" was an understatement, Michael thought. He'd done it again. He'd touched her. Drowned in her.

He'd kissed a patient, for God's sake!

He stood and moved away, gazing out across the black water. "Starting Monday, Sally will take over as your PT."

"No."

Her refusal made him turn and look at her. "I'm not in the habit of kissing my patients, Dana. I can't—"

"Dr. Stewart sent me to you," she interrupted, her voice brusque. "He said you were a specialist and that you could help me. Do you want to be the one to tell him he was wrong?" She didn't wait for an answer, but went on to state, "I'm not willing to jeopardize my chance for a full recovery because of an incidental kiss."

Incidental? Hardly. He'd felt something powerful jolt through him at the taste of her. He hadn't intended to kiss her, hadn't wanted to, he told himself, but now that he had, he knew it would be a long time before he could get it out of his mind.

He felt a stir of annoyance as he studied the determined tilt of her chin. Did she honestly think he was unfeeling enough to just shrug it off? Or had it really meant that little to her? He'd laid a part of himself open to her tonight, in more ways than one. He wasn't sure he liked the feeling of vulnerability that went with that.

"All right," he heard himself say. "We'll do it your way this time."

A light breeze swept up from the river and she shivered.

"You're cold," he said quietly. "Let's go back to the car."

"On the surface, Sarah Gordon is just another statistic in this country's long history of drug abusers. It's what Sarah did for a living that makes her death stand out.

"She was a top cardiologist at Los Angeles General Hospital.

"She frequently performed open-heart surgery.

"She was a drug addict."

Dana sat in her darkened office, still wearing the clothes she'd gone to dinner in, and read the article she'd called up on her computer monitor. She'd needed to know. Not for the *Gazette,* or the assignment, but for herself. It was old news, long forgotten by the public, but it was still very much a part of Michael.

And that made it important to her.

She'd subscribed to the on-line news system as a research tool. By tapping a few keys on her computer she had access to the morgues, or clipping files, of major metropolitan dailies and regional papers across the country. She could find out anything she wanted to know about a given town or city by reading several years' worth of its local newspaper, and do it very quickly. In this case, she had an approximate location and year. It hadn't taken her long to find what she was looking for.

She tapped a few more keys and read, "Sarah Wentworth-Gordon had been killing herself for years with amphetamines. An autopsy revealed evidence of advanced coronary-artery disease. She was killed by drug abuse. But more important, she was killed by her profession."

There had been complaints filed from two other hospitals, Dana discovered, and Sarah had resigned once. No action was ever taken, no sanctions given. The article referred to a code of silence among physicians. "Don't point a finger." "It's not worth it." "It's too risky." "Encourage the doctor to go to another hospital where he or she will be somebody else's problem."

Sarah Gordon was under investigation for a complaint made against her by one of her patients at the time of her death.

"Her husband, Michael Gordon, director of physical therapy for the same hospital, refused to comment."

It appeared that not a single detail had been left out. There was even a brief history of Sarah's life as a child in Carson City, Nevada—something that served no real purpose to the focus of the article, but had become common practice in the mainstream press.

Dana searched the files for more information, but there had been no follow-up story. She sat up and rubbed the back of her neck. Sarah Gordon's death had been a tragedy, for her, for the hospital, and for the lives she might have saved had she lived. But it was Michael who still suffered.

A surge of anger welled inside Dana. It had been a needless death. All it would have taken was for one of the hospitals where Sarah had worked to step forward and offer to help her overcome her addiction. Instead, they'd turned their backs, afraid of "rocking the boat." And now Michael was shouldering the guilt.

Dana exited the news system and called up her word-processing program.

"I make the slow, painful journey to the basement of East Ridge Hospital," she wrote. "I stand in the doorway of the physical therapy center, my hands tight on the walker I need to support me. I hide behind dark glasses, not wanting anyone to see my depression—a weakness nearly as debilitating as my injury. After the last of three operations on my badly damaged left knee, I wait to start the physical therapy I know I must have if I am ever to walk normally again. Near terror grips me."

Dana felt as if she were writing about someone else. She shuddered, remembering the pathetic, bitter woman she had become. She'd been certain that her previous PTs were deliberately torturing her, trying to break her down and make her cry. But her stubbornness had kept her eyes dry and her chin up.

Until Michael. She'd been telling the truth when she said she didn't want to jeopardize her chances of recovering by switching physical therapists. She'd be lying if she said that was her only reason.

"He is a tall, imposing man, with a muscular build—a marathon runner—and director of the physical therapy center. He is to be my physical therapist, and I find him intimidating. It will be his job to teach me to accept my injury, to deal with the pain, not wallow in it, and to show me how to walk again."

Who had helped Michael deal with *his* pain? she wondered.

"By instinct and training, he sees through my defenses. Afraid to surrender what little control I have left, I fight him. 'When you fight me you defeat yourself,' he tells me. His logic is inarguable, but it only makes me resent him that much more."

Dana remembered how furious she'd been with him when he'd told her to take two aspirin and leave her dark glasses at home.

"I can't treat you if you don't let me see what you're feeling."

What was *he* feeling?

She didn't understand why he had kissed her. Perhaps it had been out of loneliness—the simple need to hold and be held that the memory of his loss had stirred.

Dana knew that for her it wasn't that simple. He was capable of shattering her senses with no more than a brush of his lips. The havoc he could wreak if he ever asked for more was beyond her comprehension. The knowledge that he never would ask for more hurt worse than knowing he still didn't trust her.

Steven came over the following morning to take her grocery shopping. He carefully avoided the subject of last night's dinner, but she could see him watching her out of the corner of his eye as he drove her to the store.

She met his gaze once and he looked away, shifting uncomfortably on the pickup's bench seat. She knew he was dying to ask how it had gone.

Let him sweat a little, she thought.

"You're too quiet," he finally blurted.

She gave him a frosty look. "That was a rotten thing to do, Steven."

"I can't help it if Bev made other plans."

"You knew she had other plans before you set up dinner—if this woman even exists. That's why you made the reservation under Michael's name instead of your own. And don't bother trying to lie your way out of it. I always know when you're lying to me."

"How?"

"Your ears turn red."

As if to prove her point, Steven's ears turned crimson. He glanced at himself in the rearview mirror and muttered an oath. "All right, I confess." He looked at his reflection again and shook his head. "Jeez."

"I've told you before to stay out of my love life," Dana said.

Steven shot her a quick glance, his brows raised. "So there *is* something between the two of you."

"That's not what I meant," she snapped, flustered.

"Come on, sis. Don't try to tell me you two weren't about to kiss when I walked in on you Friday."

Dana looked straight ahead.

"Now whose ears are turning red?"

"They are not!"

"No, but your cheeks sure are. Sorry, sis, it must be hereditary." He downshifted to make a corner, then said, "You may not be aware of it, but for the past two weeks the dominating subject of our conversations has been Michael Gordon."

"He's my PT."

"You never talked about any of the others, unless it was to criticize their mental capacity."

Dana laughed despite herself. "All right, I admit there's something about him that I find...interesting." She tossed him a quick glance and added, "That doesn't mean there's anything going on between us." Her lie brought the heat back to her face, and she turned to look out the side window.

Steven chuckled. "Yeah, right."

Dana didn't argue with him. She couldn't deny the tenuous bond that had been formed as a result of the things Michael had shared with her. Last night she'd seen a man she had the feeling few people really knew. He was complicated and compelling.

She wasn't afraid of him anymore. Her greatest fear now was that she *had* become emotionally involved.

Chapter Nine

Michael stared at his image reflected in the glass of the patio door. He wore no shirt, his muscled arms hung loose at his sides and his jeans rode low on his narrow hips. He studied his reflection with a critical eye. He was at his strongest now, his muscles firm, tendons resilient. He had the kind of strength that came with years of training and discipline. Yet at the moment, he felt hopelessly weak, overpowered by a five-foot-seven creature with a flowing black mane and clear blue-green eyes. He'd gone to dinner with her last week because it had been important that he understand her, necessary in a way he couldn't define.

And now she knew more about him than he'd ever told anyone before. She didn't seem to be aware of how naked that made him feel.

He'd been a fool to let her talk him out of turning her care over to another PT. Trying to think of Dana as only a patient took a tremendous amount of willpower. More than he seemed to possess, he was forced to admit by week's end. Every minute he was with her, the more they talked and laughed and argued, the harder it became to ignore how he felt about her. His ability to focus on the job was nonexistent when she was near. She was the most frustrating, determined, fascinating woman he'd ever had the pleasure, and curse, to meet. His better judgment told him to forget about her, before either of them got hurt.

Listening to his better judgment didn't seem to be one of his strong points lately.

He turned away from his reflection and went into the living room, to the glass-fronted entertainment center, where he selected a cassette of assorted classical music. Adjusting the volume to a moderate level, he stretched out on the sectional and tried to relax.

That was something else he didn't seem to be very good at lately.

It wasn't supposed to be like this. *He* was supposed to be the strong one, the one in charge, affected by a woman only when and if he chose.

He snorted at his own egotistical imagination. For his own peace of mind, he was either going to have to snap out of this romantic delusion he seemed to be caught up in, or turn Dana's care over to Sally and be done with her.

It sounded simple.

He closed his eyes and listened to the music. Musetta's waltz, from *La Bohème*, was playing—a sweet, smooth-flowing piece—perhaps his favorite. There had been a time when he'd thought of taking waltz lessons. The idea of gliding across a dance floor with a beautiful woman in his arms had appealed to him. He'd mentioned it to Sarah once, and she'd laughed at him.

"When would we have the time?" she had wanted to know.

Never. There had never been enough time. But the desire was still there.

Did Dana know how? he wondered.

As the music continued to play, he imagined a large ballroom with a multimirrored globe rotating from the ceiling, casting colorful points of light over a dimly lit dance floor. He saw himself in a black tux and white silk shirt with a satin bow tie at his throat. Dana wore a long whisper blue evening gown that scooped low in the back, the satin fabric hugging her firm, rounded breasts and the curve of her slender hips. Something simple and alluring. When he placed his hand at the small of her back, her bare skin would be smooth to his touch.

They had the dance floor to themselves. Even the source of the music was indiscernible. Dana turned and put her small hand in his. He imagined the fingers of her other hand twined in the hair at the nape of his neck. A shiver coursed down his spine at the thought. With a gentle pressure he pulled her to him. He already knew how her slender curves would feel.

She was pliant and graceful in his arms as she followed his lead. When she tilted her head back to look at him, her mesmerizing blue-green eyes sparkled and danced in the whirling reflected light. Her long raven hair brushed his hand at her back, and he wrapped his fingers in it. He knew it would feel like silk.

She rested her cheek on his shoulder, her breath warm at his neck. He drew her tighter against him. The sway of their bodies moving in rhythm together was starting an exquisite ache in his groin.

Cupping the back of her head with his hand, he turned her face to his and captured her mouth. He knew how she would taste, sweet and intoxicating. Was she like that all over? His hands found the satiny fabric at her shoulders and eased it downward, over her breasts, her hips, her long slender legs, until it lay like a soft blue cloud at her feet. He pulled his mouth from hers and imagined her standing naked before him. She would be beautiful, he had no doubt. He'd seen her cheeks flush with emotion. Would the rest of her do the same when he touched her?

He ached to find out.

She would undress him, slowly at first, her fingers loosening the bow tie at his throat. His jacket would fall to the floor, joined by the black satin cummerbund from around his waist. She would tear at the buttons of his shirt, exposing his bare chest to her kisses. Then his trousers would fall into the pile of discarded clothes and she would be in his arms again, bare skin touching bare skin. He would explore her lovely body, taste it, caress it, until she trembled against him. He wanted her arms curled around his neck, her long legs locked around his hips, her soft skin sliding over his, as he buried himself in her. They would follow the gentle rhythm of the music until passion took over, dictating a primal beat all its own.

So engrossed was he in his sensual imaginings, that when the cassette deck shut itself off, the sound made him jerk. He lay on his back in the darkened room, staring at the ceiling. It took him a moment to realize that the dance hall, Dana, and their passion, had all been a product of his imagination.

A fantasy. An incredibly realistic one.

His body's reaction was testimony. He may not have had a woman in a long time, but it was apparent that all his parts were in full working order—and eager to be put to use. He shifted to ease the friction of his jeans, but the ache persisted. It wasn't just any woman he wanted; it was Dana Whitaker.

Uttering a sound of frustrated disgust, he rose and went upstairs.

Dana settled on the couch, her pajama-clad legs propped on the end of the coffee table, and a cup of coffee cradled in her lap. She tried not the think about the fact that in a few minutes the Grand Floral Parade, the Rose Festival's showcase event, would begin its four-and-a-half-mile journey through downtown Portland. Syndicated television coverage would bring the parade to millions of households in over a dozen states. Newspaper reporters and photographers would be there to record it, as they had done for the past eighty-plus years. And for the first time in her six years as a journalist, she wouldn't be a part of it.

Not being there to share in the excitement and wonder on children's faces, or to feel the nervous electricity generated by the thousands involved in putting the event together—the more than one hundred floats, bands and other entries that would celebrate this year's theme, "Simply Send Roses"—took all the fun out of it for her. So on this first Saturday in June, she was going to watch Bugs Bunny.

She barely glanced at the newspapers scattered at the other end of the couch, or the layer of dust that coated the tabletops. She didn't have the energy. Sleep had been elusive, punctuated by dreams of Michael. She'd made a mistake in insisting that he continue as her PT. In the past week, they'd discussed everything from the weather to politics. Safe topics. Even then, they'd had their disagreements, but she'd been surprised at the number of things they had in common, as well. Despite her best efforts to think of him as just her therapist, it was getting harder and harder to ignore the feelings she felt developing inside her. The more she learned of him, the more involved she became. For her own sake, she should probably stop asking questions.

She'd finished the article Val had assigned her to write. It had become an obsession. She'd thought maybe by finishing it, she'd be able to get him out of her system, put her feelings in a neat little file as she'd done the story.

Fat chance.

She sipped her coffee and tried to focus on the antics of Daffy Duck as Robin Hood.

The doorbell rang.

"Rats," she grumbled. She set her coffee down and grabbed for her crutches. "This had better be good."

She made her way to the door and slid the peephole cover aside.

"Ohmigod."

Michael's rugged profile, slightly distorted by the viewer, made her heartbeat accelerate with nervous excitement and panic. *What's he doing here?* She looked down at her oversize pink pajamas with their faded teddy bears and worn knees.

"Ohhh," she moaned. Her mind raced. Was there something she'd forgotten? How fast could she dress?

She looked through the peephole again and saw him reaching for the doorbell an instant before the sound made her jump.

"Just a minute!" She ran her fingers frantically through her tousled hair and almost lost one of her crutches. It was hopeless.

With a sigh of resignation, she unlocked the dead bolt and grabbed the doorknob. "If this doesn't scare him, nothing will," she muttered. She put on her brightest smile and opened the door.

"Michael! What a surprise!"

He stood with his hands shoved partway into the pockets of his jeans, his Levi's jacket hanging open over a snug black T-shirt. He gave her a crooked smile as he took in her attire. Dana didn't know whether to die of embarrassment or faint from the effect he was having on her pulse. Instead, she stood in the open doorway, an unnatural grin pasted on her face, wishing he'd say something.

"Did I wake you?"

"No. I was just, uh, watching cartoons." She tried running her fingers through her hair again. This time her crutch got away.

Michael caught it in one deft move and handed it back to her. God, she looks good, he thought, marveling at how seductive those silly PJs were on her. She looked like she'd just gotten out of bed, with her long black hair cascading in loose disarray over her shoulders and no makeup to detract from her porcelain cheekbones and full ruddy lips. Sleepy and natural. He thought about how much he'd enjoy taking her back to that bed. It would be a long time before either of them got any sleep, that was for damn sure! He shifted from one foot to the other, swearing silently at himself for responding like a walking hormone.

Dana mistook his action for impatience. "I'm sorry. Where are my manners? Please, come in." He stepped past her and into the cluttered living room. "I apologize for the mess. I—I wasn't expecting company."

Michael knew that was his cue to tell her what the hell he was doing there. For a fraction of a second, he asked himself the same thing. Then he turned and looked at the sight she made in her pink teddy bears.

"I know I should have called first," he said, "but I suddenly got the urge to go to the Rose Parade, and I came by to ask you to go with me."

Dana gave a short, incredulous laugh. "That's very considerate of you, but the parade starts in just a few minutes, and I'm—" she glanced down at her pajamas, the color in her cheeks deepening "—not dressed."

Michael shrugged. "We won't miss that much."

"We won't get within a mile of the parade route," she corrected.

"I've got that taken care of," he assured her. "There's a place I go that no one else knows about."

Her look was skeptical. "Where?"

"That's a well-kept secret," he said with a grin. After all his careful preparation, he was going to feel pretty foolish if she didn't go along. And if she did, would she be angry when she found out he'd tricked her?

"Why me, Michael?"

His expression became serious. He sucked in a deep breath and let it out slowly. Enough with the games. "We need to talk," he told her.

"I agree."

"Please come with me."

"Give me ten minutes."

She was ready in nine. Wearing pull-on jeans, a loose-fitting pink sweatshirt, and her slip-on canvas shoes, she brushed her hair and pulled it away from her face with two bright pink combs, then added a little color to her already flushed cheeks.

There were some breaks in the clouds as they headed toward the downtown area. Michael had put the top up on the BMW. In the confined space, Dana could breathe in the subtle male scent that was exclusively his.

She gave herself a mental shake. It was bad enough that her mind wandered when she was alone. It was worse when he was so close.

"What did you want to talk about, Michael?"

There was a faint tightening of his jaw before he answered. "You know this isn't working, don't you?"

Dana looked out the side window. "Yes, I know," she replied softly and wondered if they were talking about the same thing. She ventured a glance in his direction. The tightness was still there. "You're uncomfortable working with me."

"Uncomfortable?"

His short, harsh laugh only confirmed Dana's fears. In his eyes, she was still a reporter.

"Starting Monday, Sally will take over as your therapist," he stated.

"I understand."

"Good." But Michael had the feeling she didn't understand at all.

"You were sure I'd put up an argument, weren't you?"

The resentment in her voice was evident. He surprised her, and himself, by replying, "I'm not sure of anything when I'm around you."

Seconds ticked by, long and silent.

"This isn't the way to the parade," Dana realized aloud.

"I know."

Since he seemed intent upon keeping their destination a secret, Dana sat back and took note of where they were. The Laurelhurst district in southeast Portland—stately old homes, tree-lined streets, a huge park that sat in the heart of the residential neighborhood. She'd often admired the area's charm.

Just beyond the park Michael turned again, and Dana came to the conclusion that one of these beautiful homes was his. An instant later, he pulled into the driveway of a two-story white stucco that sat back from the corner above a low, ivy-strewn rock wall. Terra-cotta tiles covered its steeply pitched roof and sculptured arborvitae flanked a long, recessed porch. A wooden trellis laced with grapevines formed a canopy over the driveway.

Michael shut off the engine. "This is where I live."

"It's lovely," Dana acknowledged.

"I'll understand if you're angry with me."

"I'm not angry, Michael."

"I wanted you to see my home," he explained, not quite looking at her.

"Why?"

He sat very still. "You wanted to know more about me. It seemed like a good place to start."

Dana couldn't be certain, but she thought she'd just heard him imply that he wanted to trust her. "I'd like that," she whispered.

For the first time since parking the car, he looked straight at her. There was relief in his smile. "Then let's go inside."

A narrow flight of brick steps led from the driveway to the porch. Dana maneuvered her crutches through the cramped space with Michael's steadying hand at her back. On the porch, he unlocked the wide oak door and pushed it open, standing aside to let her go ahead of him. As she stepped inside, her gaze skimmed over the polished hardwood entry, a banistered stairway, ivory walls and fawn-colored carpeting, coming to rest on two lawn chairs and a TV tray laden with popcorn and fruit in the middle of the room.

She jumped when Michael reached around behind her with a remote control in his hand and aimed it at the square-screen television. The sights and sounds of the Grand Floral Parade came to life. Dana's laughter bubbled over the noise.

"I promised you a parade," he said, his mouth whisper-close to her ear.

She turned and met the playful glint in his eyes. That and his nearness drew the breath from her. "You really put a lot of thought into this." Her voice was faint. His gaze had dropped to her mouth, and she felt herself lean toward him, anticipating his kiss.

Michael cleared his throat and stepped back. "Let me take your jacket."

Dana recovered enough to shrug out of her light-weight rain parka. Michael hung it on the bentwood coat tree next to the door, then took off his own jacket. Dana watched as he hung it beside hers. She liked the way his T-shirt accentuated the muscles in his back and shoulders.

When he turned around and met her gaze, she boldly told him, "You look good in black."

His mouth lifted in a crooked smile. "And you look good in pajamas." He leaned forward and touched his lips to the corner of her mouth, then retreated before she could register that he'd kissed her.

"Come in and make yourself comfortable."

Dana was thankful for the support of her crutches as she made her way across the room. Michael had the unnerving ability to make her weak in the knees. She sat in one of the lawn chairs and laid her crutches on the carpet beside her.

"Can I get you something to drink?" he asked. "Coffee? Orange juice? Beer?"

"Coffee would be nice. Black."

He disappeared through an arched doorway. Dana took a deep steadying breath and looked around the room. Behind her, a dark brown sectional curved in an L against two walls with a brass floor lamp at each end. There was a large fireplace made of gray stone and a framed poster of Mount Hood hanging over the oak mantel. To the right of that was an entertainment center, stereo and TV. Simple, almost stark. Somehow Dana couldn't imagine Michael spending much time here.

Michael stood with his head in the refrigerator and inhaled the chilled air. Dana hadn't been in the house five minutes and he was already having a hard time keeping his thoughts clear. Maybe this hadn't been such a good idea, he mused, with an edge of sarcasm. It could get damned embarrassing if he had to keep running to the kitchen.

Muttering an oath over his lack of self-control, he grabbed the milk and slammed the refrigerator door shut. Moments later, he made his way back to the living room with two mugs of coffee, one dark, one light.

"Have I missed much?" he asked, handing Dana a mugs.

"Thank you." Her gaze darted to the television. "Just some commercials," she said in answer to his question. The reality was she didn't know what he'd missed because she hadn't been paying attention.

He settled into the chair next to hers. "Are you comfortable? Can I get you anything else?"

"Yes to the first and no to the last," she replied, smiling. "Watch the parade."

He did. He was like a child in his fascination with the elaborately adorned floats, marching bands and drill teams from across the country, equestrian entries decked out in silver and bright Western gear, clowns, dignitaries—he was entranced with it all.

And Dana was entranced with him.

"It's quite a challenge to get so much color and detail from strictly organic materials," she explained in answer to a question he had about the floats. "It takes a lot of work and patience, hand-pasting individual flower petals, or grains, or whatever nature can provide to achieve just the right effect."

Michael listened in awe.

By noon the popcorn was gone and coverage of the parade had wound to an end. Michael picked up the remote and shut off the TV. "That was fun," he said, grinning at her. "Thank you."

Dana returned his smile, a little confused. "Why are you thanking me?"

"For being here to share it with me." His mouth took on a wry twist. "And for not getting angry over being lured here under false pretenses."

She considered his ruggedly handsome face. "I have the feeling you don't have any trouble luring women into just about anything," she stated, but it came out a little huskier than she would have liked.

There was a faint sadness in his sudden laugh. "I wouldn't know. You're the first one I've tried it with."

Dana sat motionless, staring at him, while her heart hummed in her chest.

Michael looked away, picked up a Golden Delicious apple and worked it between his hands, all traces of his smile gone. "After Sarah's death, I swore I'd never get close enough to anybody to get hurt like that again," he admitted quietly. "There hasn't been a woman in my life since."

It was the bleakness in his eyes when he turned and looked at her that got to Dana first. She'd had glimpses of it before, but never without some other harsher emotion to mask its impact. Before she allowed it to overcome her, there was one thing she needed to know.

"Why, when you have such an obvious dislike for reporters, am I here?" she asked.

"I didn't ask the reporter. I asked the woman."

"The reporter *is* the woman, Michael."

He took his time returning the apple to the bowl. "Maybe it was to prove to myself that I'm not afraid of you."

"Afraid of who? The reporter or the woman?"

"I don't care that you're a reporter," he said, although he still wasn't comfortable with it. "It's what you do to me, the way you make me feel, that scares me. I don't have any control over it."

"How do I make you feel, Michael?"

He let himself touch her, just a light stroke of the pulse that throbbed along the side of her throat. The fantasy he'd had last night flashed through his thoughts, hot and alive. "I feel like carrying you up those stairs and making love with you the rest of the afternoon,'' he admitted, his voice heavy with emotion.

"What's stopping you?''

It came out as a breathless whisper that Michael understood. Her pulse raced beneath his fingertips. "I'm not into one-nighters. We need to spend some time getting to know each other first.''

"Then why won't you continue as my PT?''

"Because I've lost my objectivity.'' He studied the fullness of her lips. They clouded his concentration, and he drew his gaze back up to hers. "I feel for my patients, Dana, but I don't let those feelings get in the way of my judgment when it comes to their treatment. I'm having trouble doing that with you.'' He pulled his hand away. "I find myself second-guessing my decisions. Am I being too easy on you? Too hard? It's not fair to you, and it's driving me crazy. Hell, I don't even know that I'm ready to commit to a relationship with you or how you feel about me.'' His voice had an edge of exasperation to it. "All I know is I can't go on touching you and pretend not to feel anything.''

Her mouth opened, then closed, as if his admission had left her at a loss for words. When she finally did speak, her voice reminded of a sultry summer evening.

"I'm not sure what I'm feeling right now, either, Michael. But I'd like the opportunity to find out.''

It was intended to be an easy kiss. He drew his hand through her hair to the back of her neck and tipped her mouth up to his. He'd thought that having tasted her once, he'd be ready for the impact this time. Her lips touched his and he knew he was mistaken. There was an urgency in the way she returned his kiss that drove caution out the door. His fingers tightened in her hair, and he met her passion with a hard hunger of his own.

He'd meant what he had said about wanting to make love to her. Here. Now. But he knew if he did, it would be over between them before it even started. Physically he was ready—God, how he was ready!— but emotionally he still had a lot of fear to work through.

He allowed himself the pleasure of one last, long taste, before he pulled away. He felt as if he'd run ten miles—winded and exhilarated.

It was a moment before Dana opened her eyes. When she did, she looked stunned. Michael gently stroked her cheek as he pulled his hand back.

His smile brought a deep rose color to her skin. "I think I'd better take you home now."

Chapter Ten

Dana liked Sally. She'd had some misgivings when she went in for physical therapy Monday afternoon. Sally was young and bubbly and petite. She couldn't possibly be as good as Michael was.

Nobody could, Dana realized with chagrin. Like it or not, she was hooked on the man. Her thoughts seemed to center around him, instead of on the independence she'd been striving to regain these past months. She'd begun to question her desire to be on her own.

Maybe she would have been more comfortable with her attraction if she knew what Michael was hiding from, why he was afraid of his feelings. He'd told her he didn't want to get hurt in a relationship, and she could understand that, even sympathize with it. But there was more to it, something he wasn't telling her.

She wouldn't allow herself to fall in love with a man who wasn't being completely honest with her.

And she was uncomfortable with the way her heart plummeted when she entered the PT center and he wasn't there.

"Hi, Dana," Sally greeted. Her short auburn curls bounced as she approached, her small mouth curved upward in a cheery smile. Today she was dressed in purple knit pants and a matching textured sweater. "How are you feeling this afternoon?"

Three weeks ago Dana would have found the young therapist's vitality depressing. Now it made her smile. "I'm fine," she answered. "And you?"

Sally rolled her eyes. "I'm too busy to think about it! Let's use this mat," she said, pointing to the one behind Dana. "I guess it'll take me a while to adjust to these new hours," she went on to explain.

Dana moved to the exercise mat and sat down. "New hours? Has Michael taken some time off?"

"Michael?" Sally laughed. "Not likely. He's working the early shift and training in the afternoon. Lie back, and let's see what you can do."

"Training for what?" Dana questioned from her supine position.

"The Cascade Runoff," Sally's experienced hands moved over Dana's knee as she spoke. "It's in three weeks."

"Yes, I know." Part of the Rose Festival, the fifteen-kilometer race through downtown Portland was scheduled for the third Sunday of the month. Dana hoped to cover the event, as she had in years past.

"I'm surprised he didn't tell you. Bring your leg back toward your chest as far as you can. Bend your knee."

Dana pondered Sally's comment as she brought her leg up. Why hadn't Michael mentioned it? she wondered. Had it slipped his mind?

Or had he been afraid she'd start asking more questions?

"This'll be his second year to compete, you know."

"No, I didn't know that." Dana slowly lowered her leg. "How did he do the first time?"

"I think he said he came in fifteenth."

Dana's eyes widened in spite of her unsettling train of thought. "That's not bad when you consider almost eight thousand runners competed."

"You're telling me. But he talks like it's no big deal. Guess you could say he's the strong silent type."

Dana suppressed the caustic remark that came to mind, but it was difficult.

Sally moved off the mat. "Sit up," she instructed, "and let's see what you can do with the weights."

Dana put her feet on the floor and watched as Sally wrapped a two-pound weight around her left ankle. "How long have the two of you been working together?"

Sally's brows knit. "Let's see.... About seven months now." She adjusted the Velcro fastener. "How does that feel?"

Dana twisted her foot back and forth. "It feels good."

"Okay. Show me how high you can lift it without straining."

Dana lifted her weighted foot off the floor. "Do you like working with him?"

Sally gave a merry laugh. "That doll? Who wouldn't." Her gaze shot up and met Dana's. "But don't worry." She stuck her left hand out and flashed the small diamond on her third finger. "I have a man of my own. We're getting married in December."

"Congratulations." Dana smiled.

"I didn't want you to think I was the competition, if you know what I mean," her young therapist explained.

"No, I'm not sure I do."

"Well, it's obvious that you and Michael have a thing for each other." Sally grinned at the sudden color Dana felt rising in her cheeks, and continued, "I saw it the first day you walked in here."

When Dana stopped moving, Sally put a hand under her ankle and said, "Try to do a couple more."

Dana brought her foot up. "What did you see?" she questioned hesitantly.

"Sparks," Sally said, her brown eyes glinting. "I've seen Michael get tough with a patient before, but there were *sparks* flying between you two."

"Sparks?" Dana gave an incredulous laugh. "I wanted to strangle him!"

"I know." Sally grinned and removed the weight. "First you hate them, then you start to like them a little." She paused and gave a wistful sigh. "Then you fall in love."

Michael felt his way through the darkened study to the desk. It was Wednesday night. Late. He should have been in bed hours ago. Switching on the goose-neck lamp, his eyes focused on the copy of the *Mult-nomah County Gazette* lying on top of a stack of files. A flash of panic twisted his stomach. Dana had left it for him at the PT center that afternoon. He wouldn't have seen it yet if he hadn't gone back for some notes he'd forgotten.

It was almost midnight, and he had yet to drum up the courage to open the paper and read the article she'd written.

He sat at his desk and looked around him at the small paneled room he called his study. An array of books on running and body dynamics, and some ac-tion-adventure and science fiction filled the wooden crates he used as shelves. A fake Indian rug covered the hardwood floor and ivory blinds the room's one window.

He'd bought the desk, a battered oak dinosaur, at a thrift store. He didn't have to worry about nicks or rings on the finish, because it came with them. Right now it was covered with patients' files, notes to him-self, more books, and an old black dial telephone, an-other thrift-store find. It was the only place in the three-bedroom house where he was truly comfort-able.

Until tonight.

Swearing under his breath, he grabbed the paper. The story he was looking for was in the second sec-tion. Partners In Pain. An interesting choice of words, he mused. There was a color photo of Dana leaning on her crutches, a pensive smile on her face. He studied the photo—the way she seemed to be looking at him, her head tipped slightly and her long raven hair draped over one shoulder. It amazed him how the mere act of looking at her could make him ache. He stared at the photo for a long time before going on to read what she'd written.

He was caught up in the story with the first sentence. It was concise, insightful, sometimes painfully honest. As he read, he found himself getting a look into the feelings of his patients that he'd never had before. He got to see what they thought of him, as well as the struggle with depression, the battle of wills between patient and therapist, and finally the confiding, sometimes grudging, bond that developed between them. It was obvious that the author had experienced the things she wrote about.

He came to the end of the article and slowly laid the paper down. There *was* a bond between them, one that went beyond patient and therapist. He'd shared a part of himself with her. It hadn't been an easy thing to do. And it probably hadn't been very wise. But it couldn't be undone.

Partners in pain. Is that what they'd become?

His gaze traveled the room—his private, tranquil domain. He'd never noticed until Saturday, after he'd taken Dana home, how empty it was. He longed for her presence to fill the emptiness in his life. He'd deliberately rearranged his schedule so he wouldn't see her at work. He'd needed the space to think. But he hadn't realized how much he'd miss her.

He searched through the clutter for the telephone. Setting it in his lap, he leaned back in the chair and put his bare feet on the corner of the desk. He dialed her number and absently stroked his mustache while he waited for her to answer.

"Hello?"

Her voice was groggy and muffled, as if she were lying in bed and had her face to the pillow. Michael wondered if she slept on her stomach. He remembered her teddy-bear PJs and felt a tender, gentle tug.

"I'm sorry I woke you," he murmured. "I forgot how late it was."

He heard her shift in bed. "Michael? Is anything wrong?"

He felt another tug at the concern in her voice. "Everything's fine," he assured her. "I wanted to let you know how much I liked your story."

"You read it. I'm glad."

Michael massaged the bridge of his nose and sighed. "I also want to apologize, Dana."

"For what?"

"Doubting you. I was wrong not to trust you."

"Thank you, Michael. That means a lot to me."

The sexy huskiness in her voice made his skin tingle.

"You really enjoyed the article?" she asked.

Michael smiled to himself. It felt good to know that even though she didn't need his approval, it was still important to her. "Yes. I like that you wrote it from your viewpoint. I feel like I understand my patients, and you, a little better now."

"What did you learn about me?"

Her question skimmed across his heart. "I learned that behind those dark glasses and that tough exterior was a tender, frightened woman," he answered softly.

"I'm not frightened anymore, Michael."

No, but *he* sure as hell was. The feelings that coursed through him ran too deep. "That's good," he whispered. "I hated knowing you were afraid of me."

What seemed like a long space of time, but was actually only seconds, passed before either of them spoke, and then it was Dana who broke the silence. "Why didn't you tell me you were competing in the Runoff?"

Several more seconds ticked by before Michael answered. "I guess I was still afraid of you," he admitted. "Afraid that you'd want to write about it."

"I do, you know. It'll be big news when you win."

Michael's hearty laugh filled the room. He liked the sound of it. He liked that Dana could bring it out of him. "You seem pretty sure I'm going to win. Do you know something I don't?"

"Just a feeling I have."

He could hear the amusement in her voice. "An American hasn't won that race in ten years," he informed her.

"Which means your victory will be that much sweeter."

Again, Michael laughed. "Okay," he told her, "if I win the Runoff, you can have an exclusive."

"*When* you win," she corrected. "Michael? Are you sure this doesn't make you uncomfortable?"

What made him uncomfortable was knowing that soon he'd have to hang up, and he didn't know when he'd see her again. "I'm sure, Dana. Will you have dinner with me tomorrow?"

"I thought you were in training."

"I still have to eat."

Dana laughed. "All right. Dinner would be nice. Thank you."

"I'll pick you up around six, if that's okay," he said. "And wear something casual."

"Six, casual. Anything else?"

"Yeah," he murmured, a contented smile pulling at his mouth. "Get some sleep."

She chose a pair of pull-on denim slacks, a lavender cardigan with a V neckline and three-quarter-length sleeves, and her old standby canvas shoes. It took her three attempts to get her hair to satisfy her. She tried to convince herself that she wasn't the least bit excited about having dinner with Michael again so soon, but her trembling fingers proved otherwise.

He arrived promptly at six, wearing blue jeans, a navy T-shirt and running shoes. The casual look definitely suited him, Dana thought, trying not to appear too happy to see him.

She failed miserably.

"It's good to see you again, Michael."

The corner of his mouth lifted in a crooked smile that took her breath away. "Hi, beautiful. Are you ready?"

She nodded.

He took her to a small sandwich shop in the southeast area that he frequented. It wasn't fancy, but long and narrow, scrunched between the buildings on each side of it. The wood floors were worn light blond in spots and the high ceiling left the heating and exhaust ducts exposed. A coat of whitewash gave it a clean, bright look. Framed black-and-white prints of Europe hung on the walls. Red checkered cloths covered the small tables, and the delicious aromas of pastrami, French bread and fresh-brewed coffee filled the air.

Dana was delighted with it, and that was all that mattered, as far as Michael was concerned. He was enjoying just being there with her, seeing her smile and the way her eyes took on the lavender hue of her sweater.

He ached for wanting her, but there was more to it than that. When it finally struck him what it was, he almost laughed. He was comfortable with her! It was a new feeling. Life with Sarah had been a roller coaster ride of emotions, brought on largely by her drug addiction and his inability to understand what was happening. Dana, on the other hand, was like an island in the sea, a haven where he felt safe.

They ordered turkey on rye and homemade minestrone soup. Afterward, they sipped espresso.

"How are you and Sally getting along?" Michael asked.

Dana's cheeks flamed. She tried to cover it up by taking a drink of coffee and nearly choked. Michael watched her with a knowing smile on his face.

"She's been giving you a bunch of romantic notions about you and me, hasn't she?" he drawled.

With a short laugh, Dana set her cup down. "Sounds like you know her pretty well."

"She's young and in love and thinks everybody else should be, too."

"That's Sally." Dana toyed with the handle of her cup. "I like her. She's fun to be around, and she's a good PT."

"Well, I never thought I'd hear you say that."

Dana looked up and saw the grin on Michael's face. She matched it with one of her own. "Are you jealous?"

Michael laughed loud enough that a few of the other diners turned and looked. "No, I'm not jealous, Dana. I'm pleased that you've gotten your confidence back."

She gave him a radiant smile that intensified the ache of desire plaguing him. He picked up his espresso and drained it in two gulps. It scalded his throat, effectively taking his mind off his libido. Setting the cup down, he glanced at Dana and saw her watching him with raised brows.

"Would you like another cup?" he asked, even though he could see she hadn't finished the first one.

"No, thank you."

He ordered another for himself, knowing that he would be climbing the walls later from the caffeine. But it was easier than trying to explain what had gotten into him.

Dana sipped her coffee until his arrived, then said, "I'll be glad when I can start driving again. Steven hasn't said anything, but I know taking me back and forth to therapy has been an inconvenience."

Michael took a swallow of the bitter liquid, suppressed a grimace, and pushed the cup away. "You can start driving any time you feel ready," he told her. "You're physically capable of it now."

"Do you really think so?" she asked. There was nervous excitement tinged with disbelief in her voice.

"There's no reason you can't start easing back into the things you used to do. Sally and I both agree that your progress has been very good. In fact, I think you should consider going back to work soon."

Dana stared at him as if he'd just spoken to her in a foreign language. "You can't be serious."

"There must be things you can do at the paper that don't require a lot of footwork," he said. "And you'd work half-days at first, so you don't overtire yourself. I think it would be good therapy."

"You *are* serious."

Michael saw the turmoil in her expression. "What's wrong? I thought that was what you wanted."

She gave a short laugh and shook her head. "It is! I guess I never thought I'd actually get there, is all."

"You've had a rough experience, Dana, but the worst of it's behind you."

A slow smile lit her features. The combination of that and the caffeine in Michael's system made his pulse drum.

"Steven was right. I couldn't have done it without you."

"That's not true," Michael said emphatically.

"It is," she argued. "You were the only PT stubborn enough to put up with me."

Michael's brows shot upward. "*Me* stubborn?"

She laughed, thoroughly enjoying herself. "Would you prefer obstinate?"

Dana liked the deep resonance of Michael's laugh and the way his eyes crinkled at the corners. He was so at ease with himself, confident without being conceited or domineering. When he was with her, he made her feel like she was the center of his attention. She found herself wondering what kind of lover he'd be.

"So would you like to give it a try?" he asked.

Dana felt the blood rush to her face. "What?"

"Driving," Michael said, eyeing her curiously. "Would you like to give it a try?"

"I...I don't know." She scrambled to get her thoughts on the same track as his. "My car was repaired, but it's a manual transmission. How would I work the clutch?"

"We'll worry about that later. First, let's see how you feel about getting behind the wheel."

"I'm afraid I don't understand."

"You will," he promised, smiling.

He paid the bill then and together they strolled outside. The cool evening air felt wonderful on Dana's heated skin. The tops of the trees and the surrounding buildings were cast in a warm orange glow as the sun dipped low in the sky.

The BMW was parked against the curb at the end of the block. When they reached it, Michael turned and handed Dana the keys.

She stared at them, then at the beautiful white convertible. "I couldn't."

"You wanted to start driving again," he reminded her, "and this is an automatic. You won't have to use your left leg at all."

"You don't understand."

Michael studied the troubled look in her eyes. "Are you afraid of getting hurt again?"

She frowned and looked away. "No, it's not that."

"Do you feel like I'm trying to force you to do something you're not ready for?"

She shook her head in exasperation. "No!"

Michael raked his fingers through his hair, feeling a little exasperated himself. "Help me out here, Dana. Why don't you want to drive my car?"

She turned and looked at him. "Do you know what my Volkswagen looked like after the accident?"

He shook his head, but from the expression on her face, it must have been bad.

"A squashed soup can," she confirmed.

"And you're afraid the same thing will happen to my car if you drive it."

She bit at her lower lip and looked away.

"That's crazy. Do you know what the odds are of something like that happening?"

She still wouldn't look at him. He moved closer and gently took her chin, turning her face to his. He gave her a crooked smile and said, "I'm insured."

"Oh, that makes me feel a lot better," she remarked, her voice arid.

But it was the look of hurt in her expression that had Michael regretting his flippant words. "All I meant was, it's just a car."

"But it was your wife's car!" she blurted.

Michael let out a heavy sigh. He looked into Dana's eyes. In the fading light, they were a deep shade of lavender that he found very intoxicating. "I didn't keep that car to remind myself of Sarah," he assured her, his voice soft. "I kept it because it was more practical than the gas hog I'd been driving. Sarah's here." He put his hand over his heart. "That car means nothing more to me than a way to get around."

"Are you sure?"

"I'm sure," he murmured. He kissed her forehead, her nose, and finally her mouth. She tasted of espresso, dark and sultry.

After a long moment, he pulled back and said, "How 'bout taking me for a ride, beautiful?"

Dana clenched the leather-covered steering wheel and leaned forward slightly in the seat as her eyes darted from the road ahead, to the side streets and driveways, then to the speedometer. She was going ten miles an hour under the limit. Cars sped by as if she weren't moving.

Getting into the driver's seat had been easy. She had enough mobility in her left knee by now that it wasn't difficult to get comfortable. Michael had helped her get her crutches in and adjusted the seat for her shorter legs. And with no clutch to operate, she didn't need her injured leg to drive with.

A sleek black car honked its horn as it whipped around the BMW. Feeling foolish, Dana pressed down on the accelerator, bringing the car up to speed. Everything seemed to rush at her then. There were so many places to watch at once, so many places a car with a drunk driver could come speeding out of.

"Relax, Dana," Michael spoke softly from the seat next to her. He reached over and began to massage the back of her neck.

Dana expelled the breath she'd been holding and tried to smile at him without taking her eyes off the road. She made a conscious effort to loosen her grip on the steering wheel while taking deep breaths. Michael's blunt strong fingers expertly kneaded the tight cords of her neck until she couldn't help but relax into the comfort of the bucket seat, her fears fading with the half-light of dusk.

"Better?"

This time when she smiled at him it was an easy, almost-content movement of the lips that made Michael's pulse pound. He pulled his hand away, afraid she would feel it through the tips of his fingers.

"Have you given any thought to getting something you can drive temporarily?" he asked.

"I suppose I could drive Mom and Dad's car for a while. It's stored in my garage until they get back from Europe," she explained. "They told Steven and me to feel free to use it while they were away. And it's an automatic."

She signaled to turn. The sporty convertible responded like the well-tuned machine that it was. Dana realized she was actually beginning to enjoy herself.

"Of course, it's not nearly as nice as your little car," she said, "but it'll get me around." She smiled and tossed him a sidelong glance. It pleased her to see that he was smiling, too, and seemed completely relaxed with her driving.

She pulled up to her house and shut off the car's engine. "Thank you, Michael." She released her seat belt and turned to look at him. "For everything."

He'd already released his seat belt and was leaning toward her. "It was my pleasure."

His words were a warm rush of air on her face. Dana focused on the area just below his mustache and unconsciously moistened her lips.

"Let me," he offered. He nipped at her lower lip, testing its soft fullness, and heard her intake of breath. Cupping the back of her head, he tilted it just enough to comfortably fit his mouth over hers. He knew he was treading dangerous waters, raging and deep and hot. He didn't care. Her mouth moved against his, demanding more, and he didn't think about how complicated this could get. Instead, he thought about a man and a woman seducing each other on a deserted dance floor.

He pulled back to catch his breath, but stayed close enough that his lips brushed against hers when he asked, "Do you waltz?"

She drew back and gave him a look of mild surprise. "Not lately," she answered.

"But you do know how?"

Amusement sparked in her eyes. "I took some lessons a few years ago. Why do you ask?"

Michael's gaze had dropped to her mouth. Her lips were parted and still swollen from being kissed. "I'll explain later," he whispered, and claimed their sweetness once again.

After a languorous moment, she pulled away and murmured, "Would you like to come in?"

Yes! He wanted to relieve the throbbing ache of need she'd set to flame deep inside him. He wanted to find out if she was as sensual as the raven-haired beauty in his fantasy. Her kisses told him she would be.

"It's getting late, and I have the early shift tomorrow," he heard himself say.

Disappointment and something else—the knowledge that there would be another time when she wouldn't be as patient, perhaps?—flashed across her expression.

Michael accepted it and said softly, "I'll walk you to the door."

Chapter Eleven

Dana pressed her foot to the accelerator of her parents' midsize sedan and thrilled at the sense of freedom it gave her. Not since her fifteenth birthday, when her father had taken her for her first driving lesson, had being behind the wheel of a car felt so wonderful.

Wearing a midcalf rayon skirt, its tiny floral print the same sky blue as her long-sleeved knit top, her hair pulled back from her face with silver combs, and just the slightest color added to her lips and cheeks, she knew she looked as good as she felt. After six long months, she was finally going back to work!

The twinge of fear she'd felt earlier over breakfast had all but disappeared. She'd had some misgivings about jumping back into the work force after such a long hiatus. Would she be able to handle all of her assignments? Working just half-days, would she be able to turn out the amount of copy Val expected from one of her "star" reporters? She glanced at the single crutch leaning next to her on the bench seat, proof of her continuing improvement. She was getting around pretty well now, but there were still things she couldn't do.

She shoved her negative thoughts aside, determined not to let them spoil her exuberance. She turned into the *Gazette's* lot and was surprised to find her old parking spot empty. She had a sense of coming home as she pulled into it and shut off the car's engine. With nervous anticipation, she grabbed her crutch and purse and made for the employee entrance at the side of the old brick building.

She knew something was wrong the minute she stepped through the door. There weren't the sounds of frenetic activity that there should have been in a newspaper office on a Monday morning. The thump of her crutch on the hard linoleum floor and the swish of rayon against her nylons echoed in the large room. She stopped and looked around her.

The entire newsroom was crammed with file cabinets and desks, those in the center for four reporters, two photographers and a secretary, with others along one wall, separated by low partitions, for the managing editor, features editor, and advertising and circulation managers. The glass-walled corner room was for the editor-in-chief. It was Val's office.

And everything was just as Dana remembered it. Papers, photographs and books were piled everywhere. Cartoons and notes were tacked helter-skelter on walls and partitions, or taped to the sides of computer monitors. Steam rose from foam cups sitting precariously amid the clutter.

There were other signs of habitation—jackets and a sweater hanging on the coatrack, a purse stashed under one of the desks, monitors left on. After-shave and perfume mingled with the smells of fresh coffee and yellowed newspaper articles.

Maybe they're in a meeting, Dana thought, glancing at Val's office. The blinds were closed and the door shut, which was odd. Meetings weren't usually secretive.

Then it occurred to her what was going on, and she smiled. "All right, you can come out now!"

There was scuffling and a furtive "Shushhh!" from behind the door.

She moved closer. "Come on. I know you're in there." Turning the knob, she opened the door a crack and peeked in.

"Surprise!"

Crammed into the tiny office was the entire staff, their familiar faces cheering and laughing. A computer-generated banner on the wall behind the editor's desk welcomed her back in bold headline lettering, and a multitude of balloons seemed to fill every space that a body didn't.

Someone bounced a yellow one off her nose. She gave a startled laugh and turned to see who it was.

"Welcome back, Danny," Peter greeted her with a hesitant smile.

His wheat-colored hair was neatly combed, something of a rarity for him, and his maroon necktie was snug against his throat. In fact, his entire appearance was more tidy than Dana remembered it ever being before, and she was touched to think he might have done it for her.

She gave him a warm smile. "Thank you, Peter. It's good to be back."

Marla, as impeccable as ever in a vermilion outfit, stood off to one side. When Dana met the younger woman's ice blue gaze, she knew there was one person in the room who wasn't happy to see her return and that, as far as Marla was concerned, their rivalry was still very much alive. Dana held her gaze and deliberately smiled to confuse her.

"Val said you needed to put on some weight."

She turned at the familiar voice of Luther, the circulation manager. Squat and balding, he pushed his way to the front of the group. In his stout arms was an enormous box of assorted doughnuts.

Dana laughed as her gaze searched the room for Valerie.

"She's hiding behind her desk," Judy, the paper's other photographer, informed her.

"Thanks a lot, Val!" Dana shouted.

"Don't mention it!" came Val's reply from the back of the room.

"You're going to share those, aren't you?"

It was Graham, the journalist who had a desk next to Dana's. Everybody laughed. Graham ate continually and remained as thin as a twig stripped of its bark.

"Of course," Dana told him, "but touch the maple bar and Ted will be writing an obit for you in this week's edition!"

It was pandemonium then, as her co-workers shuffled by with words of welcome, asked how she was feeling, then grabbed a doughnut and made room for the next person.

Everyone but Marla. Dana saw her march from the room, her full ruby lips pressed together as if disgusted by the whole display.

Dana fielded more questions and endured a few hearty pats on the back, before catching a glimpse of Valerie standing behind her desk.

"Okay, people!" Val boomed. "I hate to spoil the party, but we have a paper to put out!"

It was music to Dana's ears.

Within seconds, there was no one left in the office but Dana and her editor. Balloons lay everywhere. The box of doughnuts on the desk was empty, except for one maple bar.

Valerie swatted a red balloon out of her chair and sat down. "That goes for you, too, kiddo."

"Thanks, Val."

"It was their idea," her friend said. "If I'd had my way, we wouldn't have bothered with all this foolishness." She plucked another balloon off her desk and batted it toward Dana with a smile.

"They're a great bunch, aren't they?"

"Yeah. Now take your maple bar and get to work."

"Right, chief!"

Dana was surprised at how easily she slid into the routine—like putting on a favorite pair of well-worn shoes. Everyone made sure she was kept busy. The weekly newspaper hit the stands on Wednesday morning and everything had to be ready to go to press by Tuesday. No sooner had she finished copyediting one story, than another one was tossed in front of her.

She looked up occasionally to breathe in the excitement that was in the air, the mystery and power of the printed word like a tonic to her senses. Again the feeling of having come home washed over her. Her coworkers were her family. She could see Luther over the partition around his desk. The top of his head was a bright pink as he carried on a heated conversation with someone over the telephone. Ted discussed a photo layout with Judy, and Graham sat at the desk next to hers, his Adam's apple sliding up and down his long throat as he read to himself from his computer monitor and shoved another doughnut into his mouth.

Her gaze moved down the line of desks to the one at the opposite corner where Marla sat chewing on the end of a pencil and reading. Every family had an undesirable relative or two, she thought ruefully. It embarrassed her to think she'd actually envied the woman.

A shadow fell across her desk, and she looked up to find Peter standing next to her with a foam cup in his hand. He set it on the edge of her desk and said, "I thought you could use a refill."

Dana smliled. "Thanks."

"How's it feel to be back?"

"Like I was never gone."

Peter stuffed his hands into the pockets of his tweed slacks and looked around the newsroom. "Yeah, the place never changes." His gaze came to rest on Dana again. "How are you doing? You're not getting tired or anything?"

"No, I feel great."

"You look great, too."

Dana's mouth quirked. "Don't you think you're laying it on a little thick?"

He chuckled. "What can I say? It hasn't been the same around here without you, partner." He pulled his hands from his pockets and rested them on the edge of her desk, leaning close. "Now that you're back, somebody else can work with Ms. We'll-do-it-my-way-or-not-at-all," he said, keeping his voice low.

"Has it really been that bad?"

His face contorted, making Dana laugh softly. The old camaraderie was still there, she realized.

"Let's just say Marla and I differ on a great many things, including what makes a good shot."

"If you've got something to say to me, Peter Holister, be man enough to say it to my face!"

Dana and Peter looked over at Marla. She'd put her pencil down and was glaring at them.

Peter straightened and regarded her with a big grin. "I was just telling Danny how stunning that particular shade of red is on you."

Dana had to turn away to hide her smile.

"Don't you have anything better to do with your time than waste it trying to be cute?" Marla retorted. She dismissed them both with a parting narrow-eyed look.

Peter thrust his hands into his pockets and sighed. "I'm heartbroken."

Dana snickered.

He looked down at her and shrugged. "Win some, lose some." Then he smiled. "I almost forgot. Val wants to see you in her office before you go."

"Go?" Dana glanced at the electric clock over the water dispenser and discovered she'd already worked five hours and would be late for physical therapy if she didn't leave soon.

Peter laughed at her startled expression. "Welcome back to the rat race, Danny."

Michael felt a little stupid sitting on Dana's front step like an infatuated teenager. He knew one of her neighbors across the street was keeping an eye on him, because the curtain in the picture window would pull to one side a few inches, then drop back into place when he swung his head in that direction. He just hoped to God whoever it was didn't call the police before Dana got home.

He tried to justify his reason for being there. As Dana's PT, it was his job to make sure her first day at work went smoothly. Except that he wasn't her PT anymore. He looked down at the white paper bag beside him. Fragrant steam rose from its contents. She might be too tired after work and therapy to fix herself a decent meal. He was merely looking after her health.

Bull.

The simple truth was, he wanted to be with her. He realized he wasn't being fair. She would expect more from him than he could give. He'd told her almost everything about himself and his past. Everything but the most important thing—the reason he could never commit to a permanent relationship.

But she was driving him crazy. He couldn't concentrate on his work or his training. Sleep had become an iffy proposition. And that damned fantasy plagued him day and night. He figured the only way he was going to get any peace was to see her, satisfy whatever it was that had grabbed his insides and refused to let go.

Maybe the intensity wouldn't last, and they'd be able to walk away without regrets. Right now, that didn't seem very likely, but it was the only thing he had to cling to.

He heard a car turn into the driveway and looked up. When he recognized Dana behind the wheel of the sedan, his breath caught. Feeling like an infatuated teenager, he shook his head and stood to greet her.

Dana pulled in beside the BMW and parked. He looks magnificent, she thought when she saw him. He was wearing a black T-shirt again and faded Levi's that rode low on his hips. He stood with his legs shoulder-width apart and his thumbs casually hooked in the front belt loops of his jeans. She didn't know why he was there, but a tremor of excitement rippled through her at the sight of him waiting for her. She glanced down at the pink sweats she'd changed into for therapy and wished she had put her skirt back on. She grabbed her crutch and got out of the car.

"How was the first day?" he asked as she made her way toward him.

"It went very well," she said, then laughed at her own calm. "It was terrific!"

"I'm glad." He smiled and touched her cheek. "I thought you might be tired, so I brought dinner. How does Chinese food sound?"

"Marvelous," she breathed. He pulled his hand away and her breath returned, reluctantly. She'd hoped he would kiss her. It was something she'd thought of often.

He picked up the paper bag and followed her inside. She turned toward him as he pushed the door shut. He was standing close enough that she could make out the aromas of shrimp, stir-fried vegetables, ginger... and a hint of musky after-shave.

She closed her eyes and inhaled. "Mmm... smells delicious. I'll make some tea."

"It can wait a minute."

Michael cupped her chin in his free hand and brought her mouth up to his. There was nothing timid about his kiss. He knew what he was doing—what he'd wanted to do for days. He doubted the food would have much flavor after he'd had a taste of her, but he wasn't going to let that stop him. He took his time exploring her sweetness and pulled away only when he felt his control slip almost out of reach.

"You were going to make tea?" he asked, smiling.

Michael decided he liked Dana's neat little kitchen, as he opened an assortment of small white boxes and arranged them in the center of the table. The yellow woodwork was flashy, almost gaudy, but it reminded him of sunshine. Like the woman who lived there. It was a cozy room.

He glanced over at Dana. She was taking teacups from a cupboard, her head tipped back, her long black hair nearly reaching the rounded thrust of her bottom, as she braced herself against the edge of the counter. Her pink sweatpants were snug rather than baggy. No, he corrected, *cozy* was not applicable to the feeling that shot through him just then.

"Do you take cream or sugar in your tea?" she asked as she arranged the teapot and cups on a wooden serving tray.

"No."

The distracted tone of his voice made Dana look at him. There was a flash of exposed desire in his dark eyes before he looked away. She felt the heat start somewhere low in her abdomen and rise to her face. She gave herself a moment to recover, then said, "If you'll carry this to the table for me, we can get started."

A warm, snug feeling prevailed as they dunked deep-fried shrimp in hot mustard and sipped eggflower soup. Dana came to the conclusion that it was the best meal she'd ever eaten in her small home. And the only thing she'd had to do was boil water. She didn't question Michael's being there. He made her laugh. He made her blush. It was enough that they enjoyed each other's company, she told herself. *Don't make it complicated.*

When she was sure she couldn't eat another bite, he offered her a fortune cookie.

"You first," she told him.

"All right." He broke one of the brittle cookies in half and read aloud, "Beauty and harmony are yours."

He looked up. The desire was there in his gaze. He didn't try to hide it from her this time. Dana felt a brief interruption in the rhythm of her pulse.

"What does yours say?"

His voice was lower, huskier. It had an unsteadying influence on her hands as she held the strip of paper up. "You will achieve great things with the help of loved ones." She almost told him then what she had been suspecting for some time—that she was falling in love with him. But something in his expression told her it was too soon.

"I'm glad you thought of this, Michael."

He smiled his crooked smile and said, "So am I. I missed you."

She was still trying to recover from the effect this had on her when he stood and began clearing the table. He tossed the empty boxes back into the paper bag and carried the others to the refrigerator. Dana didn't try to stop him. It was nice to be waited on. She watched him move things around to make room for the boxes and thought how natural it felt having him there, going through her refrigerator like it was his own.

Her gaze fixed on the two faded spots on the seat of his jeans as she asked, "How's your training going?"

He straightened and turned, and she suddenly found herself staring at the front of his jeans. She sucked in a breath and jerked her gaze up. There was a wry slant to his mustache.

"I'm having a problem concentrating," he told her.

"Oh? Has something been troubling you?"

"Yes." He closed the refrigerator door and came back to the table. Bracing his hands on its edge so that his face was close to hers, he said simply, "You."

Dana looked down at his wrists, feeling uncertain. "I'm sorry."

"I'm not."

Her gaze lifted and locked with his. For a long time, neither of them moved or said anything. They didn't have to, Dana decided. The keen longing she saw in his dark chocolate eyes spoke for both of them.

"Would you like to go into the other room where it's more comfortable?" she whispered.

"Yes." He straightened and held his hand out to her.

She took it and let him help her to her feet even though she could have managed by herself. Then again, maybe not, she mused, when she met his gaze and felt her knees wobble. She reached for her crutch.

"You won't need that." He put her hand in the crook of his arm. "You can lean on me."

Dana liked that idea. She wrapped her fingers around his muscled forearm and leaned into the warmth of his shoulder.

"Would you like some music?" she asked, when they passed by the stereo.

"Sure. Something soft and easy?"

"Soft and easy, it is."

There was already a cassette in the deck. She flipped it over and punched the unit on. Then she walked with Michael to the couch. As she settled into the deep cushions, a waltz began to play.

Instead of sitting beside her, Michael moved across the room, suddenly restless. The music conjured images too intimate for relaxing.

"Is this your mom and dad?" he asked, stopping in front of the pictures over the TV.

"Yes."

"You said they're in Europe?"

"Yes. What's wrong, Michael?"

He turned. "It's this music."

"Would you like me to change it?"

"No." Musetta's waltz began to play. "Yes." He raked his fingers through his hair. "Hell, I don't know." He made his way across the room toward the door. "I should go."

Dana grabbed his hand as he passed by the couch. "Please don't. Talk to me, Michael. Stop shutting me out."

He looked down at the small hand in his but didn't speak.

"You once asked me if I knew how to waltz," Dana said. "Does it have anything to do with that?"

Michael lifted his gaze to the eyes he'd fantasized about. "It's a daydream, a fantasy I've been having. You and I are waltzing to this music."

"It's the same music that was playing the day I did the sketch of you," she told him quietly.

He stared at her. Then, because he couldn't think straight when she returned his gaze with such openness, he looked down. His thumb made small circular movements on the back of her hand as he thought about what he'd say next. How much did he dare tell her?

"We're in a ballroom—alone. There's no orchestra, yet we hear music." He looked into her eyes again and sucked in a breath. "We undress each other in the middle of the dance floor."

Dana's grip tightened in his, and she stood to face him. "Then what happens, Michael?"

He gave her a crooked smile despite the erratic pounding of his heart. "I don't know. The damned music stops too soon."

The corners of Dana's mouth twitched, but the look in her eyes was intent. "We could play it again, now, and see what happens."

He gave a low growl, deep in his throat. "To hell with the music." And he pulled her into his arms.

Chapter Twelve

The fine thread of Michael's restraint snapped, and his mouth came down hard on hers, driving her head back. He splayed his hands across her back and crushed her to him. This time it was no accident that she was in his arms. He widened his stance and drew her deeper into the kiss and his body, desperate to satiate another more primitive hunger.

Dana tangled her fingers in the thick dark curls at the nape of his neck and met the demand in his kiss, her tongue vying with his. Her breasts pressed against the hard wall of his chest, and she felt his heart thud rapidly in time with her own.

Michael needed more. He pushed his hands under her sweatshirt to feel her skin, smooth and hot against his palms. He was pleased to discover she wasn't wearing a bra. He felt her moan of frustration against his mouth when her efforts to pull his T-shirt free of his jeans met with resistance. He eased his hold on her and his shirt slid up, bunching under his arms.

"Hold on," he murmured.

She wrapped her arms around his waist, and he pulled the T-shirt over his head, tossing it toward the couch and missing. He didn't give it a second's thought.

Dana found it difficult to breathe as she marveled at the gorgeous expanse of his chest. She splayed her fingers over firm pectoral muscles and the smattering of dark hair that formed a V between them. Slowly her fingertips glided downward, over his taut stomach and lower still, to the band of his jeans. She felt him tremble and looked up. His eyes were almost black with passion and focused solely on her. Compelled by them, she drew back just enough to pull her sweatshirt over her head and shake her long hair free.

Michael took a moment to look at her—the perfection of her firm, rounded breasts, her slender waist, her raven hair a wild cascade over her creamy shoulders.

"You're more beautiful than I imagined," he told her, and she gave him a shy smile that he found incredibly sexy. He spanned her waist with his hands, then brought them up her sides to stroke the rosy peak of each breast with his thumbs. They responded instantly to his touch, growing as taut and hard as that part of him still encased in denim.

Dana closed her eyes and arched her body, pressing against him with small rhythmic movements while her fingers kneaded his strong shoulders. His mouth closed over a sensitized point, wet and hot, and a convulsive shudder tore through her. He did it again, this time lightly raking his teeth over it, and she moaned. Unable to stand the sensual teasing any longer, she grabbed the hair at the back of his head and pulled his mouth to hers, demanding to be kissed.

He obliged willingly, his mouth hungry for her. Cupping her bottom in his hands, he pulled her against the unbearable ache in his groin. He wanted to feel her under him, around him, there on the carpet, or anywhere else she would have him.

His drugged mind registered a flash of light through the closed curtains, then dismissed it, his attention refocusing on the woman in his arms. Her hands had moved to the waistband of his jeans again and she was methodically releasing the buttons.

She was down to the third one when the sound of the doorbell made her flinch, then freeze.

"Ignore it," Michael growled. His mouth and tongue teased the sensitive area along her neck. "Whoever it is can come back later." His hot breath fanned her moist skin. "Much later."

His mouth coaxed her to forget everything but him. It wasn't hard. Dana wanted him desperately, totally. She melted against him, her body aching to be filled.

"Dana? Are you in there?"

She stiffened, her fingers digging into Michael's shoulders. "Dad?"

"Sis? Open up!"

"Oh, no," she groaned. "My whole family!" She looked at Michael. It wasn't fair, she thought, gazing into his dark eyes. She'd finally broken through his reserves, finally had him where she wanted him!

There was amusement in his lopsided smile. "Shall I tell them you're busy?"

"Don't you dare!" She laughed, but she felt like crying. "Help me get dressed."

He kissed her gently on the mouth, then knelt and retrieved her sweatshirt. She hurriedly pulled it on.

The doorbell rang again.

"Just a minute!" she shouted. She glanced at Michael refastening his jeans and found it hard to suppress the disappointment she felt. He looked up. The latent passion in his eyes only intensified her disappointment.

"Your family has lousy timing," he grumbled, letting her know he shared her feelings.

"They weren't supposed to be back for another week."

Michael wanted to pull her back into his arms and kiss away the regret that lined her brow. Instead he looked for his T-shirt. He was pulling it over his head when she opened the door.

"Mom! Dad! It's so good to see you!"

Dana was engulfed by loving arms and smothered with welcoming kisses. Michael took advantage of the brief chaos to comb his fingers through his hair. Watching her with her family, he suddenly felt out of place. And apprehensive. He'd been ready to make love to her, explore every inch of her, but was he ready to meet her parents?

"It's good to see you again, Mike."

Steven had managed to squeeze past the group at the door and was walking toward him. Michael knew by the look in the younger man's eyes as they shook hands, that he had already surmised the cause of Dana's delay in answering.

"Steven," he acknowledged. "How are you?"

"Fine, thanks. And you?"

Michael saw the slight lift of his brow and decided it would be a waste of time to lie. "I've been better," he admitted.

There was understanding in Steven's smile. "I apologize for barging in on you like this, but Mom and Dad wanted to surprise sis."

Michael combed his fingers through his hair again and gave a dry chuckle. "Believe me, she was surprised."

"Michael, I'd like you to meet my mom and dad." Dana and her parents had closed the door and come into the room, Dana using her father's arm for support.

Michael walked over to them. "Pleased to meet you," he said, taking Mr. Whitaker's hand. He would have known the man anywhere. He had the same merry eyes and gentle expression that Dana had captured in her sketch of him. He stood not much taller than his daughter. His stout frame was firm and trim, his black hair liberally streaked with gray.

"Call me Lloyd," he said. "And this is my wife, Eva."

Michael looked into a pair of blue-green eyes identical to Dana's and smiled. "Eva."

To his surprise, he saw the silver-haired woman's cheeks take on a light flush. Another endearing characteristic she shared with her daughter, he mused. She was a tiny woman, smaller than Dana, but Michael sensed nothing frail about her. Her handshake was firm, her skin smooth and warm.

"It's a pleasure, Michael," she said. "Dana tells us you're her physical therapist?"

"Was." He glanced at Dana. Her cheeks were the color of ripe peaches, and her full, wide lips were a deep shade of red. *As if she'd just been thoroughly kissed.* He dragged his attention back to her parents. "It's a long story."

"Yes, well—" Eva gave her daughter a pointed look, "—we have a lot to catch up on, it would seem."

Frowning, Dana turned to Steven. "You told them?"

"It sorta slipped out," he grudgingly admitted.

Michael cleared his throat, drawing Dana's attention back to him. "I have to leave," he told her.

"Don't let us run you off," Lloyd said.

"You're not," Michael assured him, even though that was the case. He liked Dana's parents, but right now they needed time alone with their daughter. And he needed a cold shower.

"I'll walk you to the door," Dana said. As glad as she was to see her parents, she didn't want Michael to go. But she thought she knew why he had to leave and didn't try to talk him out of it.

She went as far as the porch with him. They stood looking at each other for a long moment, suddenly uncertain.

"Michael, I'm—"

He put a finger to her lips. "I know," he whispered. "Me too." Then his mouth was where his finger had been, his kiss tender.

Dana was slow in opening her eyes afterward. He was so good at that, she thought. When she looked at him, his dark eyes had a wicked glint in them.

"I feel like a teenager caught necking in the car," he murmured.

Her cheeks flushed and she laughed softly. "I'll call you later."

"You'd better."

Her cheeks were still warm with color as she went inside. Her parents had made themselves comfortable, her mother at one end of the couch, her father stretched out in the recliner. Steven brought her crutch to her, then went back into the kitchen to make a pot of coffee.

"It's nice to see you've finally found a PT that you can tolerate," Lloyd said with a knowing wink.

Dana's cheeks burned.

"Father, don't tease," Eva said. She patted the cushion next to her. "Come and sit," she told her daughter. "We want to know everything that's happened while we were gone."

"Yes," her father said, suddenly serious. "What's this about another operation?"

Dana looked at the expressions on their faces, a mixture of concern and reproach, and felt all of six years old. This is ridiculous, she thought. She was a grown woman capable of running her own life. And yet she knew that their concern was born out of love.

"It's true," she admitted.

"When did this happen?"

The distress in her mother's voice tore at her conscience. "Two days after you left," she replied, eyes downcast.

"Dr. Stewart didn't say anything to us."

Dana met her father's stern gaze with resignation. "I asked him not to."

Lloyd frowned and glanced across the room at his son. "Did you know about this?"

Steven straightened from his leaning position against the kitchen entry and shot Dana a pleading look.

She sighed and met her father's gaze again. "No, Dad. Steven didn't know anything about the surgery until your plane left the ground and I was certain you and Mom were really on your way."

Lloyd's expression softened. "Danny Girl, I know how badly you felt about interrupting our vacation plans, but we're your parents. We had a right to know."

"You had a right to enjoy your vacation without worrying about me," Dana corrected.

"You're our daughter," Eva stated. "We're supposed to worry about you."

"Mom, I'll be thirty years old in a couple of weeks."

"Age has nothing to do with it."

"That's right," Lloyd said. "We don't stop caring just because you've reached a certain age."

Dana was defenseless. How could she argue with the two people who loved her the most? She looked from one to the other. "I apologize for worrying you."

Eva reached over and patted her hand. "The important thing is that you're well."

Steven came in with four steaming mugs of coffee. "Get it while it's hot," he announced.

They drank coffee and visited for over an hour. Dana told them about her first day back at the paper, and her parents offered to trade vehicles with her until she was able to drive her Volkswagen. Then they highlighted some of their adventures in Europe, the clock shops in the Black Forest of Germany, the gondola ride from the top of the Zugspitz in the Alps, the small café where they'd had lunch in Austria.

Dana sat back and listened, captivated, her gaze darting from one parent to the other. Right or wrong, she was glad she hadn't told them about her surgery. They were like a couple of kids recounting their adventures. Yet they had a companionship and love for each other that could only have come with years of sharing life together. Would she ever have that kind of relationship with a man? she wondered.

She glanced at Steven stretched out on the carpet next to the coffee table. He looked tired, his eyelids heavy. She took a closer look at her parents and thought about the hour-and-a-half drive they had ahead of them before they could relax in their own bed.

"Why don't you stay here for the night?" she offered when her dad announced that it was time to leave. "You can make the drive tomorrow when you're more rested."

"Thanks, Danny Girl, but your mother and I are anxious to get home."

"That's why we cut our vacation short," Eva explained. "I couldn't stand the thought of living out of a suitcase one more night."

Steven yawned and sat up. "Let me put the rest of that coffee in a thermos for you."

"Before you do that," Eva said, "your father and I have something we want to discuss with you. We talked about this on the flight home." She looked from Steven to Dana. "We'd like you kids to come to the beach house the weekend after next."

"We'll have a big barbecue to celebrate a certain somebody's birthday," Lloyd said, smiling at his daughter.

"And it will give us all a chance to visit longer," Eva added. She looked at Dana. "Bring your friend Michael."

Before Dana could decide how to respond to this, her mother had turned to Steven. "Is there someone you'd like to invite?"

Dana was surprised by the immediate change in her brother's expression, a kind of dreamy softening around the eyes and mouth.

"I think Beverly would enjoy a weekend at the beach," he said.

So she does exist, Dana mused, and her brother was infatuated.

"It's settled, then. We'll expect you around noon, Saturday after next."

Long after goodbyes were said, and she had her house to herself, Dana sat on the edge of her bed, trying to decide whether or not she was pleased with the sudden weekend plans. It had been months since she'd been to the coast—the weekend before her accident, to be exact. She loved visiting her parents. They were quiet, happy times. She loved the house that sat back from the beach and the constant roar of the ocean that lulled her to sleep at night.

The thought of spending two days in the same house with Michael, family or not, sent a tingle of nervous anticipation through her. She wanted him more than she'd ever wanted any man. Tonight she'd come close to having him. It was Michael she yearned to share the rest of her life with, she realized.

But what did *he* want?

Her. This evening, he'd wanted her. But would he still feel that way a month from now? A year? A lifetime? The niggling feeling that he was holding back wouldn't go away, no matter how sensual his kisses.

Maybe he was just scared. Making a permanent commitment to someone wasn't something to be taken lightly. It meant making adjustments in your life-style, someone else to think of besides yourself, cooking for two...

Would he want to spend an entire weekend with her family? She reached for the phone beside the bed. There was only one way to find out.

He answered on the twelfth ring.

"Did I wake you?" she asked.

"Dana. No. I was...taking a shower. Did you and your family have a nice visit?"

"Yes, we did."

"I'm sorry I couldn't stay."

"I know."

"For what it's worth, I like your mom and dad."

"You made quite an impression on them, too."

"Oh?"

"You're the first PT I've had anything nice to say about," she explained. "That alone impressed them." Then before she could talk herself out of it, she added, "They've invited us to spend the weekend after the Runoff at their home in Seaside—you and me, and Steven and Beverly. Dad's planned a barbecue to celebrate my birthday."

There was a long silence.

"They have a lovely house on the beach."

Still silence.

"Michael? Say something!"

"Your birthday, huh?"

"Don't ask."

His deep-throated chuckle raised goose bumps on her arms.

"I'd love to come, Dana."

It took her a moment to respond. She hadn't really expected him to accept. But he had, and her heart was doing a funny little dance.

"Will you be there Sunday for the race?" he asked.

"I wouldn't miss it."

It was late, and they both had to get up early in the morning, but she was reluctant to let him go. "I never thanked you for dinner."

"Yes, you did."

The sexy huskiness of his voice left no doubt in Dana's mind as to his meaning. The temperature in her bedroom climbed.

"I'll have to let you buy me dinner more often," she breathed.

"You won't have to ask twice."

Chapter Thirteen

Spectators lined the sidewalks along the edges of the Burnside Bridge in anticipation of the beginning of the Cascade Runoff. Dana shifted the crutch under her right arm to a more comfortable position. "Starting conditions are ideal," she jotted in her notebook. Fifty-nine degrees and overcast. Very little wind. The river below was calm. Traffic over the bridge had been diverted, and more than 7,500 runners were assembled behind the starting rope at the east end.

Dana and Peter were in position a short distance away, on the bridge itself. As Dana took notes, her gaze flicked from one runner to the next, knowing it was futile to even hope she'd find him. *There were so many!*

Peter lifted a camera to his eye and snapped some shots. Then he chose another camera, one with a tele-photo lens, and focused on individual runners.

"There he is," he said next to Dana's ear.

"Who?" She squinted in the direction he pointed.

"Michael—who else?"

His remark made her look at him. He gave a droll smile. "Word gets around. Here—" he shoved the camera toward her "—see if you can find him with this."

She put the telephoto up to her eye and toyed with the focus. After a long moment, she began to think Peter had seen someone who just looked like Mi-chael. Then she spotted him, close to the front of the pack, and her heart began a little race of its own.

Dressed in black running shorts and a white tank top with the number nineteen pinned to it, Michael was by far the best-looking runner there, in her esti-mation. She watched him take deep breaths and stretch his shoulders, while shifting his weight from one foot to the other. Some of the runners bounced in place, some paced in front of the starting rope, and some stared at nothing at all, as if their thoughts were focused inward.

Dana brought the lens back to Michael. He looked tired. Had his mind been afflicted with sensual im-ages that made sleep impossible, too? she wondered. She hadn't seen him since her parents' untimely arri-val five days ago. She'd respected his need to focus his undivided attention on preparing for today's race.

Five days of restless pillow punching and tantalizingly vivid fantasies. Leaning into her crutch, she held the camera steady and pressed the shutter button.

"Hey!" Peter made a grab for the camera. "I'm the photographer here, remember?"

Dana muttered an apology and handed the telephoto back to him. A second later she jumped at the sharp report of the starting gun. The rope fell, and the mass of runners started their move across the Burnside Bridge. The concrete-and-steel structure shook beneath their feet.

"Go, Michael!" Dana shouted, as they thundered past her. She turned and grabbed Peter's arm. "Come on! We have to get a good spot at the finish line!"

Michael knew it was crazy, but he could have sworn he heard Dana call his name. A throng of spectators clapped and cheered from both sides, adding to the sound of thousands of running shoes pounding concrete. There was no way he could have distinguished a single voice.

He'd spent the past week trying to imagine what it would be like living under the same roof with her for an entire weekend. There would be four other people in the house, little chance for any kind of intimacy. Frustrating as hell. And yet he was looking forward to it.

He was well aware of what would have happened if Dana's parents hadn't dropped by when they did. He'd thought of little else. He knew that when it did happen, when he and Dana made love, he'd never be the same. She would become a part of him, body and soul. It was inevitable. That was the way it happened when you fell in love.

He yanked his thoughts back to the race. It was important to concentrate. One wrong step could mean being trampled. The runners in front had to get out quick. He let adrenaline propel him for the first hundred yards.

He focused on his stride, paying close attention to the length. A stride that was too long, where the heel hit the ground at a point beyond the knee, was the same as putting on the brakes, making the runner work harder.

Did he love Dana?

They turned onto Broadway Avenue, and the field began to spread out. Michael was in the lead pack, a group of about twenty. He was comfortable with the position. His movements felt fluid as he kept up the ground-eating pace of the other runners. Although Broadway appeared level, they were actually making a gradual climb. Michael felt it in the tightening muscles of his legs. It was a good feeling—a feeling of strength.

As the runners neared the Terwilliger hill, pacing became critical. The hill's steep five-hundred-foot climb could tear a runner apart if attacked too hard, making the first half of the course a four-letter word: *pain*. It had been his downfall in last year's race. Michael shook the thought from his mind. He'd never make it if he allowed fear of the course to control his thoughts.

After a mile and a half, they left Broadway and ran toward the curve on Terwilliger Boulevard where the real climb began. As Michael's body kept up a steady rhythm, his thoughts turned inward. He saw himself pushing hard off his quad muscles, his stride even and smooth, shoulders relaxed, arms pumping out speed. He imagined running the entire course, each step, each breath. He saw himself crossing the finish line, the ribbon stretched across his chest as he took first place. And standing on the sidelines was his prize, a raven-haired beauty with blue-green eyes and peach-colored lips, waiting for the winner to claim them.

His legs seemed to gain strength as he held the fantasy of Dana in his mind. In reality, he was still with the lead pack, which had thinned to twelve runners. The road steepened. He sucked in deep breaths, his arms and legs working hard.

After the third mile, it began to rain. Not a sprinkle, but a drenching downpour. It felt good on his heated body. Then his eyes began to burn from the sweat that washed off his forehead. His shoes squished with each pounding step. His muscles strained to achieve what he demanded of them.

The lead pack, now numbering six, raced past the watering station at the top of the hill and began the downhill stretch. Another group of muscles took over. Another group of muscles strained and pushed. Less than five miles to go. Michael was aware of the other runners around him, the cameramen on motorcycles, the spectators, but he didn't allow himself to think about them.

At Waterfront Park, on First Avenue, two more runners fell back, and it became a race of four. The rain let up as they passed under the Hawthorne Bridge.

The crowd of spectators thickened. One of the lead runners, a man from Kenya, pulled ahead, starting his final kick. Michael held his pace, undaunted by the widening gap. He could see the finish line. He imagined Dana waiting for him.

The Morrison Bridge was just ahead. As he passed under it, he made his move. Head back, chest out, he called on every ounce of strength he possessed and quickly passed the runner who was a few feet ahead of him. That left one runner between him and the finish line. And Dana. Caught up in his fantasy of winning, he kicked harder, demanding more from his tired muscles.

The noise from the onlookers grew. He'd narrowed the gap to a couple of yards. He could see the strain in the lead runner's stride and knew the man's body had nothing more to give. With one final push, Michael lunged past him, flying across the finish line half a stride ahead. In forty-two minutes and thirty-nine seconds it was over.

The crowd went wild over his victory. Michael slowed to a trot, then a labored walk, as he fought to take in enough air to satisfy his lungs.

Over the cheering and clapping, he heard it again—Dana calling his name. His head snapped around, and he was looking into the eyes that had driven him to win.

He moved down the cooling-off lane toward her as if in a trance, oblivious to the excitement going on around him. He hadn't seen her in a week, but it felt like months. He wanted to run to her and scoop her up in his arms, but his body was spent.

She smiled at him from beneath the hood of her yellow rain parka. Soggy denim jeans clung to her slender legs. She gripped her crutch in one hand and a notebook in the other.

"Wet day for winning a race!" she shouted.

His shirt was cold and wet and plastered to his heaving chest. He felt like he had sponges for shoes, and rivulets of water dripped down his cheeks and into his mustache. From somewhere, he found the strength to laugh. "I hadn't noticed!"

The sound of a camera shutter drew his attention to the man beside her, and a stab of resentment shot through him. She'd told him about Peter. He was her partner, which meant he saw Dana every day. Michael couldn't help being jealous of that.

"Dana, I want to—"

A microphone was thrust in his face. "How does it feel to be the first American in ten years to win the Cascade Runoff?"

Michael looked around and discovered he'd been converged upon by a wave of reporters, cameramen and photographers, all wanting a word with the winner. Questions were fired at him, but all he could think about was that he and Dana were being pushed apart, and he hadn't had the chance to kiss her.

His gaze caught hers. "Have dinner with me?" He had to shout to be heard over the crowd.

"Sure, honey!" someone yelled back.

Michael grimaced, but Dana was smiling. Damn, she thrives on this stuff, he thought, and was surprised to discover it didn't bother him. It was one of the things that made her who she was.

He saw her elbow a cameraman out of her way. "Your place okay?" she shouted.

"Yes!"

Someone jostled between them, and he lost sight of her for a second. When he located her, she was farther away, holding her hand up, fingers spread.

"Five o'clock!" she yelled. "I'll bring Chinese!"

If possible, his heart pounded even harder as desire raced hot and urgent through him.

"What was going through your mind as you overtook the lead runner?"

The question distracted him for a second. He glanced at the familiar face of a local television reporter and answered, "Not *what—who.*"

When he looked back, Dana was gone. You'll see her this evening, he reminded himself, but five o'clock suddenly seemed like a hundred hours away.

Dana shifted the white paper bag to glance at her watch. She was a few minutes early. Maybe she'd caught him in the shower. Or maybe he was taking a nap. After his performance earlier today, he certainly deserved one!

She knocked again and waited a few seconds before trying the knob. It was unlocked. Pushing the door open, she poked her head inside.

"Michael?"

When there was no answer, she stepped in and closed the door behind her. Moving to the stairway, she called his name again and waited. Nothing. Setting the bag of food on the bottom step, she repositioned her crutch, grabbed the carved banister and went upstairs.

She stood in the hallway at the top, unsure. She'd never been in this part of the house before. The hall was carpeted in the same fawn color as the living room, and a window at each end gave it a bright, open feeling. The walls were papered in a tiny floral print and the woodwork painted off-white. There were four doors—two to her right and two to her left. One of them stood ajar and she moved toward it.

"Michael?"

She peeked into the room. The wide bed with its dark oak headboard and verdant comforter was empty. Curiosity prodded her to push the door open and go in. Half expecting Michael to appear behind her at any moment and catch her snooping, she took a quick look around the room that was intimately his.

The knotty wood paneling was a light pecan, giving the room a rustic look without making it dark. The almond-colored miniblinds at the window were pulled up, and she could see the park across the street. To one side of the window was a tall dresser, the same dark oak as the bedstead. Opposite it was an old easy chair, its burgundy velour upholstery worn bare in spots.

Her gaze moved back toward the bed and she saw the framed photo on the nightstand. Moving closer, she recognized Michael. He looked tan and virile and pleased with himself as he stood with his arms around a tall, gorgeous woman. Red-gold hair offset deep sapphire eyes, and beneath a short Hawaiian print skirt were perfect long legs. Dana felt a twinge of jealousy. *Sarah.* Then sorrow misted her eyes, knowing the painful path this happy couple's life together had taken. *Poor, sweet Michael.*

She turned abruptly and left the room, ashamed of herself for invading his privacy.

Once again downstairs, she retrieved the paper bag and found the kitchen. It was old-fashioned, big, with tall, glass-fronted cabinets painted bright white, and speckled white Formica counters. Tiled floor-covering gave the appearance of worn brick and complemented the bronze appliances.

Dana set the bag of Chinese food on the counter, next to the microwave, and shrugged out of her rain parka. "Michael, where are you?" she called in exasperation.

"I'm back here. On the deck."

Beyond the dining area to her right, sliding-glass doors let out onto a wooden deck and large fenced yard. Dana could hear the low hum of a motor. She followed it outside and discovered Michael submerged to his neck in a hot tub. The surface of the water bubbled and fizzed, as steam rose into the cooler, outside air. Cedar lattice provided a secluding screen around the end of the deck.

"You didn't tell me you had one of these." She sat on the edge of the tub and laid her crutch at her feet.

He gave a lazy smile. "You never asked."

Dana pushed the sleeves of her knit cardigan up and leaned over to dangle her fingers in the water. It was warm and inviting. The steam formed tiny droplets on her lashes.

Michael peered at her through half-closed eyelids. "Did you get your story written?"

"I still have a few questions to ask the champ."

"What would you like to know?"

Dana didn't hear his question; her gaze was transfixed on something she'd discovered beneath the rippled surface of the water—Michael was naked.

"Dana?"

The sound of her name made her jerk back as if she'd been caught with her hand in the cookie jar. "What?" Her voice boomed in her ears, and her gaze flew up to meet his. There was a hint of a grin on his face, and she felt her own face flame. She turned away, perturbed with herself, and with him. He could have at least warned her, given her time to prepare for the impact of seeing him naked. Her heart felt like it was trying to pound its way through her chest.

Michael lifted his arm out of the water and ran a warm, wet finger down her forearm. "I didn't mean to embarrass you," he said softly.

His touch and the sincerity in his voice made the blood surge through her veins. "I'm not embarrassed," she replied, doing her best to avoid looking at him. She had to give her pulse a chance to return to normal before risking that.

Michael hadn't planned to be in the hot tub when she arrived, but the water had felt so good on his overworked muscles that he'd dozed and lost track of the time. Despite the heightened color in her cheeks and the obvious way she looked everywhere but at him, he didn't challenge her answer.

He pulled his hand away and laid his head back. "You wanted to ask me something?"

"Yes, I— How do you feel about winning?"

"How I place isn't as important to me as how much of myself I put into it," he replied. "I don't run for the notoriety or the money."

"Yet you still try to win."

"I try to get ahead of the person in front of me."

"What did you think about when you crossed the finish line first?"

"Seeing you again."

As he had hoped, his comment made her look at him. "You're all I've thought about this past week," he told her. He braced his hands on the edge of the tub and lifted himself to sit next to her. Out of the water, his muscles felt weighted by steel cables. He muttered a soft oath and massaged his thighs.

"Are you all right?" Dana asked. She looked at him, all of him. He was more magnificent than she could have imagined—hard, lean muscled and tanned, with a pale swatch where his shorts would have been. Water licked at the seat of her jeans, but her concern was for him alone.

He looked at her out of the corner of his eye, his expression staid. "I'm getting too old for this."

Dana put a hand to his chest. His skin was warm, and his heart thudded heavily beneath her fingers. Was it the hot water, she wondered, or her touch, that caused it to do that? She trailed her fingers downward and watched the muscles in his stomach contract. An ache, primal and intense, started in her abdomen and spread lower.

"You're about as perfect as a man can get," she told him in a voice that sounded distant and hoarse to her.

He grasped her hand and brought it up to his mouth. "I'm not a superhero, Dana, and I'm far from perfect. Right now I'm weak just looking at you."

The husky whisper of his confession intensified Dana's awareness of him. The rough caress of his mustache as he kissed her palm turned every muscle in her body to warm honey.

"How secluded is this part of the yard?" she whispered.

"It's only visible from the house."

The flame in his dark eyes told her he'd read her thoughts even before she began unbuttoning her sweater. She let it fall to the deck, then wriggled out of her damp jeans and panties. The early-evening air was cool, and tiny bumps rose on her skin as she sat next to him on the edge of the hot tub. She met his gaze, and the bumps disappeared in another warm rush.

"Are you sure this is what you want?" he murmured.

She gave a soft, incredulous laugh. She didn't have the courage, at least not yet, to tell him she'd had her birth control prescription refilled weeks ago. She'd told herself she was doing it to regulate her cycle, but even then, she'd known the real reason. "I want you so much it scares me," she admitted.

He laid his forehead against hers with such tenderness that she dared not breathe. "I know the feeling."

He kissed her then, slowly, passionately. No one was going to stop them this time, he vowed. He would take his time exploring every part of her and do his damnedest to show her how much she meant to him.

He put an arm around her shoulders and slid the other under her knees, but when he tried to lift her, his leg muscles screamed and refused to hold the weight of two people.

"Damn it," he muttered, leaning into her warm body in helpless exhaustion.

"You don't have to prove anything to me, Michael." She kissed his shoulder, his cheek, his mouth, then pulled out of his embrace and climbed into the hot tub, immersing herself to her chin in the bubbling water.

Her eyes looked more blue than green. Her raven hair floated around her shoulders like a silken cape. She held her hand out to him and he laced his fingers in hers. When she gave a gentle tug, he slid into the water. His aching muscles became buoyant, forgotten, as he floated forward and reclaimed her mouth.

His hands traveled the length of her sleek, smooth body, committing every curve and dip to memory. He felt her moan against his mouth, felt the aroused peaks of her breasts as she leaned into him. He deepened the kiss. She met the possession of his mouth with an intensity that drove the breath from him, her fingers digging into his shoulder.

But she was the first to draw back for air. An instant later, she began planting tender kisses in the crescent indentations her nails had made in his flesh. Her mouth skimmed downward to his chest. Michael had the feeling he was being tasted as she sucked the moisture from his skin. Then, curling her arms under his thighs, she pulled herself beneath the surface of the water and flicked her tongue over his stomach and navel. He gripped the edge of the hot tub, delighting in her sensual foreplay

She resurfaced and shook her head, spraying water and laughing. Michael smiled at her, pleased that she was enjoying this as much as he was. Her hands glided up his inner thighs and began to explore and stroke. He laid his head back and groaned.

A delicious throbbing grew where she touched him, building until it threatened to explode. He drew in his breath and grabbed her wrists. He saw the look of uncertainty in her eyes as he brought her arms up and draped them over his shoulders.

"I don't want to finish before we get started," he explained, his voice a husky rush of air.

A knowing smile curved her lips. Her arms tightened around his neck, and she kissed him hard and long. He matched her fervor, and felt his ability to think slipping into an abyss of sensation.

"Dana, I—"

She gave her head a quick shake. "Not now," she whispered against his mouth. "There'll be time to talk later."

She was right. They'd gone beyond talking. He'd already forgotten what he'd wanted to tell her. He ached to surround himself in her, become as much a part of her as she was of him. Moving to the center of the hot tub, he cupped her bottom and drew her hips into his. She wrapped her legs around his waist and moved against him. With a tempered, decisive thrust, wanting became reality.

They moved together slowly at first, exploring the sensation of being joined. The water licked and rolled with their measured, insistent rhythm. Dana was overwhelmed by the feeling of completeness that rushed through her like liquid fire. She clung to Michael's hot, slick shoulders, his muscles knotted cords beneath her fingers, as every movement drove him deeper into her body and her emotions. Time swirled in a misty haze; coherent thought was lost in the whirlwind of her body's response to his.

Soon their need became an urgency that knew no patience, the water a tempest, carrying them further into the storm of shared ecstasy. Waves splashed their heated bodies with a sensual pulse that had Michael grasping for control. He wanted to savor Dana and the intimate link he had with her. He'd denied his hunger too long. She cried out his name in a voice that was wonderfully hoarse and his control plunged over the edge.

With a final, driving thrust, their passion crested, held them suspended for tantalizing seconds, then released them, breathless, satiated, still clinging to each other.

Michael collapsed against the side of the tub, drawing Dana with him. She rested her head on his chest and listened to the mad pounding of his heart keeping time with hers. Entwined in his arms, she felt physically and emotionally satisfied, exhilarated, and at the same time, luxuriously lazy. She'd never imagined a hot tub could be so stimulating!

She looked around and a subdued laugh rippled from her.

"What is it?" Michael asked.

"Half the water is on the deck."

"And on your clothes."

"Mmm..." Who needs clothes? she thought, snuggling deeper into his relaxed frame. She was content to spend the rest of her life right where she was. "I smell roses."

"My neighbor has a bed of them along the fence."

She gave another sigh of contentment. "How are you feeling?"

His laughter rumbled against her ear. "Pruned."

Dana raised her head and looked at him. "Maybe we should get out."

He gave her a long, drugging kiss, then growled, "Why?"

"Because—" she smiled and bit his shoulder "—I'm hungry. And you—" her mouth and tongue teased his "—need to preserve your strength."

Chapter Fourteen

Michael opened his eyes to the half-light of pre-dawn. At least he thought it was morning. He glanced over at the nightstand beside his bed to check the time and experienced a brief rush of panic at the empty space beside the clock. Then he remembered, and a lazy smile crossed his face. He'd put the picture of Sarah and himself in the drawer sometime after he and Dana had come upstairs.

He chuckled. They must have made quite a sight. His legs had gone stiff and she'd tried to support him with one arm around him and her crutch under the other. It was a wonder they hadn't killed themselves.

She wasn't kidding when she'd said he would need to preserve his strength. She'd drained him, served him dinner in front of the fireplace, then drained him again somewhere between the living room and the stairs.

When they'd finally made it to the bed, he'd thought he didn't have any more to give.

He'd been wrong. She'd touched him in ways that made him want more. He thought of her sweet, wild cries and the way she groaned his name each time they came together, each time he buried himself in her.

He rolled over to kiss her and discovered he was alone. Another rush of panic shot through him. Then he heard a movement downstairs. Dragging his fingers through his hair, he sat up. His overworked muscles protested sharply. He was tempted to lie back and try to sleep it off, but he wanted to see Dana more. And he'd been a runner long enough to know that if he didn't get up and move around, he'd regret it.

He made a quick trip to the bathroom, pulled on a rumpled pair of jeans with worn-out knees, and went downstairs. He found her in the kitchen, mopping milk off the floor with a dish towel. She was wearing one of his chambray shirts, her curves silhouetted through the thin fabric. Michael leaned against the doorway and watched her quiet concentration on her task. He realized she wasn't using her crutch. She hardly needed it anymore. He made a mental note to speak with Sally about getting her a cane.

Seeing her this way and remembering the feelings she'd stirred in him caused the wanting to start all over again. He felt a tightening in his jeans and shifted his weight to relieve some of the pressure.

She looked up and gave him such a radiant smile that he almost groaned out loud.

"Good morning," she greeted.

"Good morning."

He moved behind her and wrapped an arm around her waist to pull her to her feet. He swayed a little and cursed his weakened state.

"Michael, I'm not finished," she protested, but the laughter in her voice gave her away.

He turned her to face him, shaping her delectable curves to his hungry body. "It can wait," he said, even as his bare foot met with cold milk.

His mouth came down on hers in an endless, drugging kiss. He heard the soggy dish towel hit the floor beside his foot and felt her arms lace around his neck. She returned his kiss with a fervor that sent the blood shooting through his veins. He could get used to starting every day this way, he thought, eventually breaking off the kiss to catch his breath.

"You must be feeling better," she murmured, her body still pressed to his in an arousing way.

"Much."

She smiled sweetly. "Good. That means you can go to the store and get another carton of milk." She kissed the end of his nose. "I'd go, but I'm not dressed."

"So I've noticed." He went for her mouth again, but she pulled back.

"Please, Michael, I wanted to make you pancakes and I need milk."

The mention of food sidetracked him for a second. "Pancakes, huh?"

"From scratch."

His brows lifted. "You can do that?"

She laughed and punched him on the shoulder. "You'd be surprised at what I can do."

The corner of his mouth came up in a crooked smile. "I don't know about that."

Her cheeks turned tomato red and long dark lashes shaded her eyes as her gaze dropped to his chest. Something deeper than simple passion stirred in him.

"Hey," he whispered, making her look up at him. "Have I told you that I'm glad you're here?"

A teasing glint danced in her eyes. "As a matter of fact, no."

He growled and tightened his hold on her. "Then I guess I'll have to show you." His mouth closed over her parted lips.

After long seconds, she pulled back. "I'm sorry, Michael, but you'll have to show me later. I have to finish breakfast and get to work."

Work. He'd forgotten it was Monday. "Call in sick?" he suggested.

"I can't do that. Besides, what about you? Don't you have patients or something?"

"I've got the day off." His smile was rueful. "I've discovered that the older I get, the longer it takes me to recuperate from a race."

Her fingers traced a line around his ear and down his neck, sending an ache through him. "You do pretty good for an old man," she told him softly.

"Just 'pretty good'?"

"Well..."

She squealed when he lifted her off the floor and spun her in a dizzying circle.

"You're going to hurt yourself!"

He laughed and put her down. But he didn't let her go. She met his gaze with a flare of awareness in her blue-green eyes that made him suck in his breath.

"Looking at you hurts more," he groaned, dragging his mouth across hers.

They didn't have pancakes that morning, and Dana was very late for work. Michael wasn't the least bit sorry. Gazing down at her as she'd dozed in his arms on the sectional later, he felt a fierce need to hold her to him forever. Never let her go. That was all he wanted—to have her with him forever.

As he'd drifted into an exhausted, contented sleep, he let himself believe it was possible.

Dana glanced over at Michael as he signaled and slipped the BMW into the far-left lane of the freeway to get around a truck. It was still there, she thought, even after the incredible week they'd spent together— the surge of desire that she got whenever she looked at him; and the flush of embarrassment she experienced when she thought of her reaction to that desire. She'd done things she hadn't known she was capable of, felt things she hadn't known possible. All because of the man sitting next to her.

He'd been waiting on her doorstep again when she got home from work Monday. She'd been late because she hadn't gotten to the *Gazette* before noon. It would be a long time before her co-workers would let her forget it, too.

He'd been shopping and had bought fresh vegetables and salmon steaks. And milk. Then he'd cooked for her. They'd traded off, his house one night and hers the next. They'd done it without thinking, as if it was as natural a thing to do as falling asleep in each other's arms had been.

Dana couldn't remember ever sleeping as peacefully or as thoroughly as she did when Michael was with her—perhaps because they didn't go to sleep right away, but made love until they were both too exhausted to do anything else.

Nothing had been said about commitment or "forever," and that was all right, she told herself. She wasn't going to spoil what they had by worrying about how long it would last.

"So what did you get me for my birthday?" she asked for what must have been the tenth time. She'd been working on him ever since she'd caught him sneaking a small wrapped package into the trunk. But so far he was being frustratingly uncooperative.

"You'll find out soon enough."

"No, I won't," she said, pouting. "I'll die of curiosity first, and it'll be all your fault."

Her unwitting statement made Michael flinch. He shook it off. "All right—" he chuckled "—I'll tell you." He waited until he had her undivided attention, then said, "I got you a box."

A small frown pulled at her brow. "What kind of box?"

"A cardboard one with something inside," he answered, grinning.

"Oh, you..." She poked him in the ribs and made him jump.

"Let's listen to some music," he suggested with a laugh.

Highway 26 narrowed to two lanes, and businesses gave way to rural homes and farms. The sweet aroma of clover filled the car as they passed a field blanketed with the tiny lavender flowers. In the distance were the white stacks of beehives. Apple orchards were in full bloom, and cattle and horses grazed in thick green meadows.

Michael gave a quick glance at the light gray clouds riding high overhead. He hoped they would blow over by the time they reached Seaside. He planned to spend some time alone with Dana on the beach this weekend.

She looked like a teenager in her oversize sweatshirt and snug-fitting jeans. She'd pulled her long black hair into a ponytail at the back of her head, accenting her high cheekbones and slender neck. Her canvas shoes had come off soon after she'd settled in next to him and her thick white socks bunched at her ankles as she rubbed her feet together in time with the music.

They liked the same kinds of music. And movies. Michael had been surprised. About a lot of things. She was so easy to be with. Even when they ran out of things to talk about, they were comfortable enough with each other not to feel it necessary to fill the silence with idle chatter.

Soon they left the farmlands behind. Tall evergreens, lush ferns, and thick stands of alder closed in on both sides of the narrow highway as it climbed through the Coastal mountain pass. Saddle Mountain appeared in the distance, its double peaks shrouded in gauzy clouds. Michael had made the drive before, but today everything looked different—new and wild and alive.

When he turned north on Highway 101, Dana opened her window a crack and he caught a whiff of fresh salt air. In a few short minutes they entered the small community of Seaside. They passed an antique shop, a gas station that rented go-carts and a kite shop, its colorful displays fluttering in the gusty coastal breeze as if they would fly away.

"Take a left at the next street."

They crossed a short bridge that spanned a shallow creek. Two boys fished from the concrete railing.

"Take another left."

Michael turned onto a narrow residential street, the creek on one side, beachfront homes on the other. He caught glimpses of the Pacific Ocean between the houses.

"It's that one there." Dana pointed to a single-story house with weathered cedar siding. It was long and narrow, perched on a slight bank, with its rear section supported on stilts. The small front yard was landscaped with huge pieces of driftwood and life-size ceramic sea gulls in various stages of flight.

A four-by-four pickup and a Volkswagen were parked in the gravel driveway. Michael pulled in beside the pickup and was helping Dana from the car when the front door of the house opened, and Eva stepped onto the porch. She had her silver hair pulled into a bun at the nape of her neck and a terry-cloth apron tied around the waist of a colorful midcalf-length dress.

"Hi, Mom!" Dana called.

Eva smiled and waved. "Need any help?"

Michael shook his head. "I can manage, thanks." He handed Dana the cane Sally had given her two days ago. "Go on in," he said. "I'll get the things from the trunk."

"Are you sure you don't need any help carrying that little cardboard box you got me?"

"So you can shake it until something breaks?"

"Hmm . . . So it's breakable."

Michael laughed. "Your mother's waiting. I'll meet you inside."

He popped the trunk lid and slung the strap of Dana's overnight bag over his shoulder, tucked her birthday gift under his arm and grabbed his own bag. Eva met him at the door.

"Michael, I'm glad you could make it."

"Thank you for inviting me," he replied, smiling. He stepped inside to the aroma of boiling potatoes, chopped onions and warm bread.

Eva slipped the gift out from under his arm and said, "I'll put this with the others. Go on in and find Steven. He'll help you with your bags."

Michael went through the kitchen and into a large airy room. He gave the polished wood floor and homey furnishings only a brief glance, his gaze drawn to the wall of glass that overlooked the ocean. Elevated above the sand and tall grasses of the beach, a wooden deck extended the length of the house. Dana's father, dressed in burgundy sweats, hovered over a smoking grill. Michael detected a hint of mesquite in the air.

Steven walked toward him in faded jeans, his blue cotton shirt hanging loose and a wide smile on his face. "Glad you could make it, Mike."

Michael nodded in acknowledgement. "It's good to see you again."

Steven's smile became a smirk. "Yeah, I'll bet." He reached for the bags. "Let me put those in Dana's room until we figure out the sleeping arrangements."

As far as Michael was concerned, his overnight bag could remain in Dana's room, with him, overnight. But Eva had come up behind him and hooked her arm through his, so he kept quiet.

"Tell me, Michael, do you know how to cook?"

He looked down at Dana's mother and gave her a lopsided smile. "I manage to keep from poisoning myself."

She laughed and patted his arm. "That's good enough. I wonder if you'd mind going out on the deck with Lloyd and seeing that he doesn't burn the chicken?"

Michael glanced outside at the cloud of smoke pouring from the grill and bravely said, "I'll do what I can."

Dana emerged from the hallway, where she'd made a hasty dash for the bathroom moments earlier. She glanced out at the deck and saw Michael and her dad talking together over the grill. She stopped to watch. The sun had found a break in the clouds and shone through the glass with welcome warmth. She squinted against its brilliance and stifled a laugh when she saw Michael grab a charred piece of chicken with the long-handled tongs and eye it skeptically.

"You must be Dana," a soft voice said.

Dana turned and looked into a pair of warm brown eyes, framed by a plump, but very pretty face.

"I'm Beverly."

Dana couldn't have been more surprised. The short brunette, her shoulder-length hair pulled away from her face in a French braid, wasn't anything like the leggy, superficial beauties her brother was usually seen with. Her cheeks had a natural glow which was highlighted by the soft pink sweater she wore. She didn't try to hide her ample hips. Her light cotton slacks hugged, rather than constricted.

Her tiny feet were bare, Dana noticed with a smile. "It's a pleasure to meet you," she said.

"Thank you," Beverly replied. "I have to tell you, I was a bit nervous about coming, but now that I'm here, I feel so comfortable. Stevie has such a nice family."

Stevie? No one had gotten away with calling her big brother that since his tenth birthday.

A flame shot up from the grill, drawing their attention back to the deck. Lloyd was trying to close the cover by hooking it with the tongs and standing back from the inferno, while Michael looked on in amusement.

Beverly giggled. "Do you suppose we should rescue the chicken?"

"I think it's too late," Dana said, her own laughter bubbling over. A wonderful warm feeling came over her at seeing Michael and her father getting along so well, even if it was at the cost of dinner.

Steven came up behind the women and slipped his arms around Beverly's waist. "What's so funny?"

Beverly looked at Dana and gave a conspiratorial wink. "Maybe you should go out and see how the chicken is coming along."

"Private conversation, huh?" He nipped Beverly's earlobe, then grinned at his sister. "Okay, I can take a hint."

Dana had never seen her brother display such tenderness toward a woman before. He'd always treated his dates as so much decoration.

"You know, don't you, that Steven's a lousy cook?" she commented, once he was out of earshot.

Beverly giggled again, a light, pleasant sound. "Ever since he tried to boil spaghetti for me." She rolled her eyes. "What a disaster! It took me a week to scrape the burned noodles out of the pot."

Dana laughed. She could see why Steven was so attracted to the woman. Her sense of humor was infectious.

They watched Steven join his dad and Michael on the deck. Something he said made the two cooks respond with loud, jovial remarks. Lloyd tried to hand Steven the tongs, but the younger man stuck his hands in his hip pockets and backed away, shaking his head.

Then it was Michael's turn. He pushed the sleeves of his navy sweatshirt up and took the tongs, wielding them as if he were about to do battle.

Dana and Beverly laughed.

If she could have frozen time, it would have been now, Dana thought, with the six of them gathered around the dinner table, eating and laughing together. She was so happy she felt as if she would explode. Then again, it could have been all she'd eaten!

She gazed at the table, wide-eyed. How could there still be food left? Potato salad, tossed salad, green beans with tiny onions, kaiser rolls, steamed carrots—she'd watched everyone dig into the food with hearty appetites. Even the barbecued chicken, though somewhat charred, had been attacked with gusto.

"If you scrape off the ashes, it's not too bad," she'd remarked, sneaking a taste before they'd all sat down, for which Michael had given her hair a playful tug.

The subject of Dana's recovery had come up during the meal.

"We can't tell you how much we appreciate all you've done for our daughter," Lloyd said to Michael.

Michael shook his head. "Dana is the one who deserves the credit. She didn't give up."

"That's my sister," Steven piped in. "Stubborn as a mule."

Dana kicked him under the table with her good leg.

"Kicks like one, too." Steven chuckled, rubbing his shin.

Michael also received congratulations for his performance in the Cascade Runoff.

"It's like having a celebrity at the table," Beverly commented, beaming.

Michael groaned good-naturedly and everybody laughed.

Eventually they gave up trying to eat all the food, and Eva rose to clear the table.

"Please," Michael said, pushing his chair back, "let me get that for you."

Eva shook her head and began to collect dirty plates, starting with her own, then Michael's. "Nonsense. You're our guest."

"After the best home-cooked meal I've had in too long, it's the least I can do."

Murmuring a thank-you, Eva handed him the plates and sat down. Dana could see by the color in her mom's cheeks and the deepening lines at the corners of her bright eyes that another Whitaker woman had fallen captive to Michael's charm.

When he left the room, burdened with a stack of dirty dishes, Eva looked at her daughter and said simply, "I like his manners."

"Yes," Beverly agreed, aiming a smile at Dana and Eva, and at the same time, delivering a sharp elbow to Steven's ribs that made him yelp. "Manners are important."

Michael came back into the room to find Dana and her parents trying hard not to laugh. Steven, his ears crimson, was standing, massaging his rib cage. There was a complacent expression on Beverly's face.

Michael put two and two together and grinned.

Steven saw it and grinned back. "Let me help you with those, Mike."

"I wouldn't want to put you out."

Steven massaged his rib cage some more and glanced down at Beverly. "I think it's the only safe thing to do at the moment."

After the table was cleared, Eva suggested they go into the living room and give Dana her birthday gifts.

"Yes," Lloyd said, pushing his chair back. "And we've got pictures of Europe to show everyone."

"Now, Father," Eva scolded, "we don't want to bore them to death."

"Oh, please, I'd love to see them!" Beverly exclaimed, endearing herself forever in Lloyd's heart. Dana saw it in the way his eyes danced as he nestled the girl's hand in the crook of his arm and walked with her to the next room.

Steven and Michael took off down the hall toward the bedrooms, leaving Dana and her mother still sitting at the table.

Eva stood and offered Dana her hand. "Shall we?"

Dana smiled and took her mother's small, warm hand in hers. Grabbing her cane in the other, she followed her mother into the living room.

"You're hardly limping," Eva commented.

Dana smiled. "I know. Isn't it wonderful?"

Her mother kissed her cheek and softly replied, "Yes, dear, it is."

Dana sat at the end of the couch while her mom and dad took their customary places next to each other in his-and-her recliners. Beverly took the padded rocking chair.

Steven and Michael came in, each carrying an armload of colorfully wrapped packages, and deposited them on the coffee table in front of Dana.

"Happy Birthday, sis," Steven said, as he sat cross-legged on the floor next to Beverly.

Michael sat down beside Dana on the couch. She would never have thought it possible, but he looked almost shy as she reached for his gift first.

Her fingers fumbled with the wrapping, then the tape on the cardboard box. When it flew open, she drew in her breath. It was another box. A music box. "It's beautiful," she gasped. She pulled it free of the wrapping.

It was polished walnut. A simple rosebud of deep red and blond inlaid woods adorned the top. She caressed the pattern, then carefully lifted the lid to reveal a burgundy satin compartment. Everyone fell quiet as the tinkling melody began to play.

After a few seconds, Dana identified it. Her skin burned as she met Michael's gaze. "Musetta's waltz," she breathed.

His dark eyes had a look in them that stole what little breath she had left from her lungs.

"You remembered."

The huskiness in his voice was like a caress on her heated skin. She didn't care that her family was watching as she put her arms around his neck and kissed him. "I'm not about to forget," she whispered.

They sat next to each other in webbed lawn chairs on the deck and watched the sun dip low on the horizon, turning the clouds into pink cotton. Behind them, they could hear the others visiting in the house, their voices muted by the closed patio door and the steady pounding of the surf.

Dana wore the knit cardigan Steven and Beverly had given her over her sweatshirt to ward off the evening chill. It was made of variegated pastels and had long, dolman sleeves. Her mom and dad had presented her with a hand-carved cuckoo clock from the Black Forest and other little trinkets from their vacation.

And there was the music box. To anyone else it might have seemed a simple gift, but to Dana it meant so much more. The intimacy and thoughtfulness that had gone into its giving had been overwhelming.

She was still feeling the impact on her heart. She would remember her thirtieth birthday for the rest of her life—cherish it.

After the gifts had come the promised vacation pictures. Dana had listened with interest and envy as her parents talked about each place they'd visited—France, Germany, Austria, Switzerland. But after a while the lure of the ocean became too strong to ignore and she'd excused herself to go outside. Michael had followed soon after with two cups of coffee.

"You okay?"

His deep voice broke the silence of her thoughts. She glanced over at him, then back at the water. "What makes you ask?"

"You keep sighing."

She met his gaze then and gave a wan smile. "I miss walking on the beach."

"So do I." He stood and held his hand out to her. "Let's go."

"But, I..." She stopped and looked up at him. Her heart felt strangely tight in her chest at the sight. He called *her* beautiful, but *he* was the beautiful one. And for the past week, he'd been her lover. His gaze coaxed her to come with him, and she put her hand in his. He pulled her to her feet, then swooped her off them and into his arms. Dana squealed and threw her arms around his neck. "You can't carry me all over the beach!"

"I don't intend to," he said. He started down the flight of open steps that led to the sand below. "When we get to the hard stuff, you're on your own."

Dana kissed his cheek. It was rough with stubble and smelled of mesquite.

"Don't distract me," he warned, "or we'll get to the bottom of these steps quicker than either of us would enjoy."

She sighed contentedly and laid her head on his shoulder. She felt safe in his strong arms. His steps were sure as he carried her down to the sand. She nuzzled his ear and he stumbled.

"Dana," he said, his voice a low rumble.

"Hmm?"

"You're distracting me."

"Good."

"I thought you wanted to walk."

"I've changed my mind," she purred against his neck.

Michael carried her to a large driftwood log and set her down. Then he straddled the log so that her hip was snug between his thighs, and loosely circled her waist with his arms.

"Okay," he said, with a deceptively innocent smile, "just what did you have in mind?"

She turned to face him. "I'm sure we can think of something," she said, sliding her hands under his sweatshirt.

He recoiled from her touch. "Good God! Your hands are cold!"

Dana laughed. "Then warm them for me." Her hands dove under his shirt again.

He made as if to get away from her, then lunged forward. Tightening his arms around her in a bear hug, he propelled himself sideways off the log, taking her with him. She yelped and landed on top of him in the sand.

He was all hard muscle beneath her. She gazed into his laughing eyes and saw desire smoldering below the surface. Her heart beat faster, her hands splayed across his taut stomach. Each time she touched him it was like the first. Electricity coursed through her. She slid her hands up his chest and felt his heart racing to match hers.

Michael found bare skin beneath the layers of clothes, her back warm and smooth. At his touch, she arched into him, making him want her with an intensity that still stunned him. She gave of herself with such trust and openness that he ached. He knew he didn't deserve it, but he craved it, treasured it like something precious that might slip through his fingers.

She lowered her head and his mouth opened to her hungry kiss. He teased her with his tongue, stroked her silken skin as she surged over him, then grasped her hips and pulled her up high and hard against him. A moan of pleasure could be heard over the breakers. He wasn't sure which one of them made it.

Somewhere in the distance a dog barked, reminding them that they were on a public beach. Dana drew her head back and gazed down at him, her eyes as soft as her smile.

"I love you," she whispered.

Michael froze.

Dana felt it, saw it in his eyes, and a stab of pain wrenched at her heart. She rolled off him and sat up, hugging her knees against the sudden cold that permeated her.

Michael stood and brushed the sand from his hair. He looked at Dana's hunched shoulders and cursed himself for hurting her. He ached to pull her into his arms. But he didn't. He couldn't. He was trapped by an old guilt. He loved her, but couldn't tell her. He'd been a fool to let it go this far.

She turned and looked at him. A tear rolled down her cheek, but her voice was strong. "Why are you afraid of my love, Michael?"

He forced himself to look away. "You want something I can't give you."

"And what is that?" she challenged.

"A commitment. A lifetime." Michael felt the warmth leave his heart as reality tore away the fantasy he'd allowed himself to live in. "I'm not what you need, Dana."

"I can't accept that."

"You have no choice."

He heard her stand, felt her anger bore through his back. "Who the hell are you to make that decision?"

There were tears in her anger. Her voice shook from them. Michael tried to shut it out, but couldn't. He turned and looked at her, saw the raw pain in her blue-green eyes, and was speechless.

Her expression softened, and she moved close enough to touch his arm. "Are you still in love with your wife's memory?"

Michael sucked in a breath and let it out slowly. It was too late to turn back. He put his hand over hers, held it for a minute, then pulled away.

"Sit down, Dana. There's something I have to tell you. Then maybe you'll understand."

Without a word, she took a seat on the driftwood log again. Michael sat cross-legged in the sand at her feet, not quite facing her. Not quite touching.

Long seconds passed before he was able to say the words out loud—the words he'd held captive in his memory, agonized over, for two long years.

"I'm the reason Sarah is dead."

Chapter Fifteen

The sun was a brilliant sliver on the horizon. The sky flamed hues of orange and red, the water reflecting more muted shades. For long seconds, the only sound was that of the waves lapping the beach as the tide came in and the mournful call of a sea gull.

Dana studied Michael's profile silhouetted against the sunset, wishing she could see his face. "The newspaper article said Sarah died of heart failure," she softly remembered aloud.

"You read it." He said it as if it was exactly what he'd expected her to do.

"I did some research. I needed to know."

He looked up at her, but she wasn't able to discern anything from his expression.

"Did you think I was lying to you?"

The accusation in his voice hurt. "No, but you weren't telling me everything."

She knew she'd guessed right when he looked away.

"And what did you find out?" he asked.

"Only what you'd already told me—that Sarah's heart stopped."

"Because she wanted it to."

His remark was so sudden that Dana wasn't sure she'd heard him right.

He eliminated any doubt by going on to state with harsh finality, "My wife committed suicide."

Dana gave a small gasp. "I'm sorry, Michael. I had no idea."

"No one did."

Michael felt as if he were dredging lead weights from the bottom of a deep lake. He'd let Sarah's family and friends believe what the paper had printed. The autopsy had confirmed an excessive amount of amphetamines in her system, but it was never determined whether it had been accidental or deliberate. No one else knew about the note he'd discovered under the bed after the paramedics had left, after Sarah's body had been taken away.

He'd stood by the empty bed trying to shake the feeling of unreality that fogged his brain, when something had crinkled under the toe of his shoe—a folded sheet of pink stationery with his name across it in Sarah's scrawled handwriting. It had taken him a long time to get up the courage to touch it. Longer still to open it.

Dearest Michael,
I can't forgive myself for hurting you. I only hope
you can find it in your heart not to hate me. I'm
so tired. Know that I love you.

                              Sarah

"You never told anyone?"

Michael gazed down the deserted beach. "I didn't
see any reason to make things worse than they already were." Had it been illegal to keep it to himself?
He didn't know. He didn't care. There'd been no life
insurance, no will. "It was nobody else's business."

"And you blame yourself."

"I'm the reason she was upset that night," he answered evenly. "We had an ugly fight, and I walked
out on her." His hands bunched into fists at his thighs.
"I left her alone, knowing she was distraught, knowing there was a bottle of pills in the house." He looked
at Dana again, the controlled evenness gone from his
voice as he demanded, "Tell me I'm not responsible."

The depth of his self-reproach and suffering had
Dana fighting back the tears. He was wrong to blame
himself. She had to make him see that. "Sarah was
responsible for her life, Michael. Not you. She's the
one who took the pills."

"She wouldn't have if I had been there to watch
her."

"And would you have watched her twenty-four
hours a day?"

"If that's what it took!" Muttering an oath, he
stood and turned toward the ocean. There was caged

anger and helplessness in his stance. "I could have helped her," he insisted.

"She had to want your help."

Michael let his shoulders sag. He massaged his temples with the thumb and forefinger of one hand. Sarah hadn't wanted his help, it was true, but he refused to believe that he couldn't have done something to save her. If only he'd tried harder.

He felt Dana move up behind him. It would be so easy to turn and let her love console him. Maybe she could even make him forget for a little while.

He drew his shoulders back. "Sarah needed me and I wasn't there. I couldn't see what was right under my nose until it was too late."

"You loved her. You didn't want to believe anything like that could ever happen."

The truth of her words stabbed sharper than any blade. "And she's dead because of it," he said grimly.

He was close enough that Dana could have reached out and touched him, attempted to comfort and soothe. But her instincts told her that coddling wasn't what he needed right now.

"Life can't always be a bed of roses," she stated. "It's not like you to walk away from a challenge."

He whirled around to face her. "This isn't a game, damn it!"

"You're right, it isn't. That's why I'm not going to let you toss in the cards and count your losses like so many plastic chips. I love you, Michael. I can't just turn that off."

"I didn't want it to get this serious."

Dana made a short, rude sound. "Well, it is serious. So what are you going to do about it?"

"I've told you why I can't let what's between us continue."

"You've given me a lame excuse about some wrongly placed guilt. There were others who knew about Sarah's drug problem long before you did. If you want to blame somebody, blame them. You didn't kill your wife, Michael. It's time to wake up and face reality."

"This *is* my reality," he said harshly, giving the air a sharp jab with his forefinger. "I've lived with it for two years. *I* was the last one to see Sarah alive. *I* was the last one to turn my back on her when she needed help."

Just like you're turning your back on me now. The thought was like a bitter pill lodged in her throat. She'd lost her heart to a man who refused to let himself love. He was terrified of the emotion. The only thing that kept her from breaking into tears was the raging anger that stormed inside her. How could he do this to her? How could he charm her, seduce her, make her fall in love with him, knowing he couldn't give in return?

"Nothing I say will make any difference, will it?"

"I can't change the truth."

"Just tell me one thing. Did you ever love me?"

Michael didn't answer. Admitting he loved her, that she was the only one who could fill the empty space in his heart, would only make leaving her that much harder.

After long seconds, she turned away. "I'm going back to the house."

"Let me help you."

"No!" Dana was startled by the force of her outburst. She lowered her voice and said, "You've done enough already."

"I never meant to hurt you, Dana."

It was all she could do to keep from stumbling as she started toward the house. Hurt her? He'd taken her heart and shattered it into a million tiny pieces. It was awkward walking in the soft sand without her cane; her limp was more pronounced, but stubbornness propelled her forward. She refused to cry. Head high, she managed to cover the short distance without falling.

She was in her room, sitting on the edge of the bed, her eyes dry, when he knocked on the door a short time later.

"It's open."

He came in and for a brief moment, their eyes met. Dana was the first to look away. She didn't want to see the torment in his dark gaze. And she loved him too much to watch him leave.

He hesitated a second longer, then lifted his bag from the foot of the bed and walked out, softly closing the door behind him.

Michael kept the wheels of the BMW on the road by sheer instinct. His mind was in a lavish two-bedroom condo in the suburbs of Los Angeles. The furnishings depicted comfortable wealth, hers more than his. It had never bothered him that his wife made more money than he did. They were both successful in the careers they had chosen. And he had thought they were both happy.

At first he'd refused to believe the rumors circulating through the hospital, that Sarah was using drugs. She was too intelligent for that. She wouldn't risk her career, her life, for a bottle of pills. When he'd finally asked her about it, she'd assured him that she only took them occasionally, to help her through a long shift.

Then came the complaint made by one of her patients—incompetence, criminal neglect.

"Sarah, you have a drug problem," he'd said, confronting her in their bedroom that evening. . . .

She stood at the dresser mirror, brushing her shoulder-length red-gold hair. She was a lovely woman, voluptuous. At thirty-seven, she had it all. His heart told him there was no way she could be a drug addict. But when he met her gaze in the mirror, there was a trace of fear in her eyes.

"You don't know what you're talking about," she replied calmly.

"Yesterday you botched a routine procedure, one you should have been able to do with your eyes closed."

She slapped the brush down and turned. "Who have you been talking to?"

"I didn't have to talk to anyone. It's all over the hospital."

"Rumors? You listened to rumors?"

"They're more than rumors, Sarah. I know about the complaint made by your patient and the impending review."

"So?" Her hands gripped the edge of the dresser behind her. "They'll find me innocent and that will be the end of it. Maybe you should just keep your nose out of my business."

"You are my business. You're my wife."

"And that gives you the right to tell me what to do?"

"I'm not trying to tell you what to do. I just want to know why you're doing this. Why are you destroying yourself?"

She gave him a condescending glare. "You don't know what it's like to cut into a person and hold that person's life in your hands." She pushed away from the dresser and held her hands out as if cradling something precious. They trembled. She clenched her fingers and hugged her arms to her chest, turning away from him. "When you give that person's life back to them they treat you like a god. That's a lot to live up to."

"What happens when that person dies because you were too drugged to know what you were doing?"

"That will never happen. I won't let it."

"You won't let it?" He grabbed her upper arm as she tried to get past him. "Sarah, you've already lost control."

"That's not true," she said, wrenching out of his grasp. "I can quit whenever I please."

"When will that be? Tomorrow? A year from now? After you've killed someone? That woman could have died because of you."

"You don't know what you're talking about."

She tried to get by him, and again he stopped her. "Look at yourself," he pleaded. "You can't sit still for five minutes, you can't sleep at night, you lose your train of thought—the drugs are killing you! Don't you see that?"

"What do you know about it? Let go of me, you self-righteous..." She struggled to free her arm. When he wouldn't let her go, she slapped him.

The force of it made his head recoil. He grabbed her other arm and jerked her against him hard enough to make her gasp. He glared at her, too angry to speak.

Her eyes widened in terror and he released her, stunned by the rage that had taken control of him.

"Get out," she hissed, backing away from him.

She started shaking. He took a step toward her, wanting to apologize, wanting to hold her until the shaking stopped.

"Get out!" she screamed. "Just get out and leave me alone!"

He left the house and walked. He didn't know how long he was gone or where he went, only that by the time he returned, it was too late. Sarah lay in bed with the covers pulled up to her chin, deathly still.

The rest was a nightmare of blurred images—CPR until his arms were numb, paramedics, questions he couldn't answer, the cold feeling of unreality spreading its shadow over him.

The sound of tires on gravel, the sensation of being pulled sideways...

Michael jerked on the steering wheel and the car bounced back onto the blacktop, toward a pair of oncoming headlights. A horn blared, and he yanked on the wheel again, sending the car to the opposite shoulder. He hit the brakes and the BMW slid to a stop.

His hands shook as he turned off the engine and headlights. He stared out at the sudden darkness that engulfed him. It took a few seconds for the full force of what had just happened to hit him. When it did, he groaned and slumped in the seat, burying his face in his hands.

Everything that had been building inside him—the fear, the anxiety, the sorrow, the overwhelming sense of loss, not just for Sarah, but for Dana, as well—burst through his shattered barriers, and he wept.

Chapter Sixteen

The last Sunday of July was warm, but not uncomfortably so for late afternoon. August promised to bring more of the same. Ideal running weather, Michael told himself, as he struggled against the uneven cadence of his stride. Beneath his ragged sleeveless sweatshirt, he felt a rivulet of perspiration trickle from between his shoulder blades down to the elastic band of his black spandex shorts. Running had become a form of torture that he welcomed. If he pushed himself hard enough, the resulting pain would drive thoughts of Dana from his mind. Thoughts that were far more tormenting.

Adam ran beside him, glancing over at him often with a doctor's frown of concern creasing his high forehead. His longer stride appeared effortless, his body showing no signs of sweating beneath his white tank top and loose-fitting nylon running shorts.

Even his hair was unmussed, Michael noted with a degree of annoyance.

They circled the park three times before Adam finally asked, "What's up, Mike?"

Michael kept his gaze fixed on the path ahead. "Nothing," he breathed heavily. Too heavily. His lungs felt like they were on fire, and his pulse pounded in his ears. But it wasn't enough to block the sound his running shoes made each time they struck the pavement. *Call her. Call her.*

A sudden muscle contraction in his right calf caused him to falter, and he muttered a curse. Adam grabbed his arm, but he shook it off.

It had been a month since he'd seen Dana. He'd picked up the phone at least a hundred times, but always hung up before finishing the seven digits that would carry her voice to him. What right did he have to expect her to talk to him after the hurt and anger he'd seen in her face that night? Besides, nothing had changed. He was the same man, with the same feelings of inadequacy and guilt. But, God, how he missed her.

"Dammit, Mike, stop!" Adam grabbed his arm again and held on.

Michael was forced to quit torturing himself. He hobbled off the path and tried to walk the cramp out of his leg.

Adam let go of his arm to pace beside him. "What's the problem?" he questioned again.

"I've got a cramp."

"I can see that. I want to know why you're running like some novice," his doctor friend demanded. "You're out of breath, you're out of rhythm, and I don't know where your brain is. I feel like I'm out here running by myself. At least for your body's sake, I should be."

Michael took a deep breath and winced at the stab of pain under his rib cage. "Lay off," he grumbled.

"No, I won't. I want to know what's happened to make you come out here and tear yourself up like this."

Michael stopped pacing and glanced up at his friend. "It's not important."

"Like hell it isn't."

He would have turned away then, but Adam's hand on his shoulder stopped him. "This wouldn't have anything to do with Dana Whitaker, would it?"

The accuracy of his question caught Michael off guard. Hearing her name spoken aloud had the effect of a vise tightening on his heart. His gaze slid downward. "What makes you ask?"

"She was in to see me last week."

Michael brought his head up sharply. "Is she all right?"

"Physically, she's fine. Emotionally, I'd say she's in about the same condition you are. What happened between the two of you?"

Michael considered shrugging and saying he didn't want to talk about it. But he didn't want to lie to his friend. The truth was, he *did* want to talk about it. For the first time in his life, he felt an overwhelming need to purge his soul.

He gave a rough sigh. "How much time have you got?"

"As much as it takes," was his friend's immediate answer.

They left the park and crossed the street to Michael's house. He didn't call it home anymore. It was too cold and empty for that. They went to the kitchen, and Michael made a pot of coffee. He'd been drinking a lot of it lately. He didn't seem to have the energy he needed to get through the day without it. They sat at the kitchen table and he told Adam everything, from Sarah's addiction and death, to his involvement with Dana and the argument they'd had. Once he started talking, he couldn't stop. It was as if the floodgate to his thoughts had been opened wide and everything spilled out at once. His friend listened quietly.

When he was finished, he stood, unable to look Adam in the eye. He valued their friendship. Yet, in the year and a half they'd known each other, this was the first time Michael had ever talked about his past. Adam had never pressured him, which Michael supposed was one of the reasons he admired the man and felt comfortable around him. Now he wondered if he had jeopardized that friendship with his bomb of woes.

"More coffee?" he asked.

"Sit down, Mike."

The soft command made him look up. There was compassion in Adam's pale blue eyes. Michael sat down. "I don't know what's gotten into me," he said, raking his fingers through his tangled dark hair. "I'm not in the habit of unloading my problems on some-body else like this.''

''I know.''

Michael looked at his friend, *really* looked at him. ''Have I been that difficult?''

''Yeah.'' Adam's smile was almost apologetic. ''You're a very private man and I respect that, but I've often wondered what you were running from.''

Michæl grimaced. ''I didn't realize it was so obvi-ous.''

''Only to someone who cares,'' Adam assured him, then added on a softer note, ''Apparently Dana cares a great deal.''

''She said she loves me.''

''Why doesn't that make you happy, Mike?''

''I don't deserve her love.''

Adam gave a short, harsh laugh of disbelief. ''That's got to be the stupidest thing I've ever heard come out of your mouth.''

Michael frowned. ''It's the truth, damn it.''

''Why?'' Adam demanded. ''Because you're hu-man? Because you couldn't control your wife's des-tiny?''

''Destiny?'' Michael made a derisive sound deep in his throat. ''Are you saying that Sarah was *destined* to die?''

''Nobody can know that,'' his friend replied gent-ly. ''I don't know why Sarah's life took the path it did. We weren't meant to know those things. All I'm say-ing is that it wasn't your decision to make.''

''I should have—''

"Stop right there," Adam interrupted sharply. "You can't change the past. You're living in a fantasy if you think that dwelling on what you should have done will get you anywhere. It's a cop-out and you know it. Admit it, Mike. You're scared."

"Of what?"

"Making a mistake. Being less than perfect."

The silence that followed was ear-shattering. Michael felt a nerve tick in his jaw as he fixed Adam with a narrowed look. "Think what you want," he growled abruptly, and pushed away from the table.

He went to the open patio door and stepped out onto the deck. Dusk was taking over the day, casting long shadows across the thick green lawn. A light breeze cooled his skin and brought with it the sweet fragrance of roses from next door. The vise on his heart tightened.

He heard Adam slide his chair back. A moment later, his friend was standing beside him.

"I'm not going to hang around here and watch you flog yourself," Adam said quietly, "but answer me one thing before I leave. Do you love her?"

A shudder of longing rippled through Michael. "Yes."

"Then let her help you get over this. Come out of your fantasy world and take a chance on life, my friend. If you don't, you'll lose her."

Adam may as well have punched him in the kidneys. It would have had the same effect. It was the thought of losing her that kept him awake nights, that made food taste like sawdust to him, that defied his attempts to concentrate on things that should have been routine.

"What if I already have?" he groaned.

"What if you haven't?" Adam countered. "At least give yourself the satisfaction of knowing one way or the other. It's time to stop running."

She'd tried to help, and he had rejected it. No, he had run from it. And now he was alone and incredibly lonely. He ached for the very things he'd shunned since Sarah's death—love, companionship, a commitment. He needed. God, how he needed! The thought of never seeing Dana again—

"Adam?"

"Yeah?"

He turned and looked into his friend's eyes. He saw no blame or sympathy in them, only a desire to help. "Thank you."

Adam held his gaze for a long second, then nodded. "You're welcome. Call me if you need to talk some more." He turned to leave, then stopped. "I almost forgot. There was something Dana said that I thought you might like to know. It didn't make a whole lot of sense to me, but—"

"What is it?"

"She said the one thing she regrets the most is that you and she never got the chance to go dancing."

"I can't let this go to press."

Dana glanced at the typed sheets of paper on the desk in front of Val and recognized them as the article she had submitted that morning. She searched her brain, trying to remember what the piece was about, but drew a blank—something that happened with annoying frequency these days.

Her gaze shifted to her editor. "What's wrong with it?" she asked, hoping for the best and expecting the worst.

"Everything," Val said. She peered over the rim of her owlish glasses. "Close the door and have a seat."

Dana knew not to argue. She reached behind her and pushed the door of the office shut, then perched her denim-clad bottom on the edge of the chair in front of Val's desk. Her hands seemed to be lost, fluttering to tuck her long hair behind her ears, then skimming the front of her oversize white shirt. All of her clothes were oversize lately. She hadn't been eating well. What was the point when everything had the consistency of cardboard?

She clasped her wandering hands in her lap and looked up at her friend. "What changes do you want me to make?" she asked. She didn't care for the way her voice wavered, as if she were on the verge of tears.

It came as no surprise that Valerie detected it immediately. Her friend's expression softened. "I'll take care of the rewriting. I'm more concerned about you."

"I don't know what you mean," Dana muttered. She looked down at her hands, unable to meet Val's astute gaze.

"Yes, you do, Danny. Ever since you and Michael broke up, you haven't been yourself."

Dana choked back the laugh that rose in her throat. She was afraid that if she let it out, it would sound a bit too hysterical. "I'm all right," she said, but there was desperation in her voice. She wanted so much to believe it. She had completely recovered from her injury and was working full time now. No more crutches or cane. No more physical therapy. No more Michael.

She'd waited for him to call, convinced that he would, once he'd had time to realize how wrong he was. But with each passing day, hope had dwindled, until, out of self-preservation, she'd convinced herself that it didn't matter. She could survive without him as long as she had her memories to keep her warm at night.

Then Steven and Beverly had announced their plans to marry, and the pain came back as sharp and devastating as it had been the night Michael had walked out of her life.

"Dana?"

She blinked. "Pardon?"

"I'm strongly suggesting you take a vacation."

Dana gave an inelegant snort. "I just came off a six-month leave, remember?"

"That was because of a physical problem," Val said quietly. She leaned back in her chair. "Now you need some time to get yourself together emotionally."

Although Dana knew her friend was right, it was like telling Humpty-Dumpty to put the pieces back together again. Her life had become a fragmented, empty shell. "I need to work."

Val gave her head a sad shake. "Your job isn't doing it for you. Maybe you could paint your house or plant a garden."

A flash of panic snaked through her. Stay home? Inconceivable. He was in every room. The walls echoed the sound of his voice, the furniture his scent, the bed his heat.

Dana closed her eyes and waited for her thoughts to calm. When she opened them again, Val was watching her.

"He still hasn't called, has he?"

Dana shook her head. She'd thought of calling him. A million times she'd thought of it. But she knew that even if she convinced him to come back to her, he wouldn't be hers. Not completely. Not as long as he continued to torment himself. A superhero? No. He was flesh and blood and muscle. Mortal. With a mortal's desires and fears.

She remembered her mother's advice after she'd explained Michael's sudden departure that night at the beach house.

"Give him time. The loss of a spouse can be difficult, especially under such tragic circumstances. It's obvious he cares for you. He'll be back."

That was a month ago.

Dana could understand his sorrow, but he was letting the past control his future. *Their* future. It infuriated her. It saddened her. And she was helpless to do anything about it.

"I just need a little more time," she told Valerie, yet there was an undercurrent of doubt in her words. Would any amount of time be enough?

"What you need is a nice long cruise," her friend gently persisted. "Put some meat on your bones, get some sun and forget about Michael."

Forget? If only she could. She swallowed, knowing she was defeated. "All right, Val. You're the boss."

"I'm also your friend, Danny. I'm only doing this because I'm worried about you."

"Don't be," Dana said stiffly. "If I can recover from a shattered knee, I can certainly get over a little rejection." Then, realizing her bitterness was misdirected, she met her friend's gaze and said, "I'm sorry. I don't mean to take it out on you."

"I'd like to wring Michael's neck for hurting you," Valerie offered.

"You'll have to take a number," came a deep masculine voice from behind Dana.

She turned and he was standing there, his tall figure framed in the doorway. He wore faded jeans and a blue flannel shirt with the tails hanging loose. He looked thinner, the lines around his mouth etched a little deeper. There was uncertainty in his stance. Dana felt her heart lodge in her throat.

He'd spoken to Valerie, but his dark brown eyes were locked on her. "Hello, Dana."

She stood, slowly, afraid he was an apparition and would disappear if she made a sudden move. She hesitated to even breathe.

Seeing her standing there, Michael wondered why he'd stayed away. She was beautiful. Small and fragile looking. It was an illusion, he knew. He'd never met a woman as strong as she was. He wanted to touch her, smooth the troubled line between her gently arched brows.

"May I come in?" he asked when she didn't speak.

"Certainly." It wasn't Dana, but the professional-looking redhead behind the desk who answered. She ose and came toward him with her hand extended. "I'm Valerie Evans."

"Michael Gordon."

"Yes, I've heard a lot about you."

Her meaning was clear. He had hurt a friend of hers, and while she was willing to be congenial, Michael knew she wouldn't easily forgive him.

"It's a pleasure to meet you," he said, taking her offered hand in a firm shake. The gold bangles on her wrist made a soft metallic sound.

"Thank you." She studied him for a long moment, then released his hand and glanced over at Dana. "If you'll excuse me, I have business to take care of. Feel free to use my office."

"Thanks, Val." Dana waited until the door closed before looking at the man standing within arm's reach of her. Questions raced through her thoughts. *Where have you been? Have you been as miserable as I have? Why didn't you call? Do you love me?* They all went unasked as she stared at him. He was gorgeous.

"I've missed you," he said.

"You could have called," she answered, unwilling to admit that she'd missed him every bit as much. But now she longed to reach out and touch him.

"I wanted to, Dana, but I needed . . ." *You. I need you.* "Time." He sucked in a deep breath, and her fragrance, clean and fresh, filled him. If he could only touch her. "I don't expect you to forgive me," he said, "but I want you to know how sorry I am for hurting you."

It wasn't what she wanted to hear. Not even close to it. She turned away, but there was nowhere to go in the cramped space. "Is that why you're here?"

"I had to prove to myself that you were real." Talking with Adam had made him realize he'd been deceiving himself. He'd been avoiding life for fear of making a mistake, of being human, by living in a world of what might have been. A fantasy. He didn't want that to be all he ever had of Dana. And then because he didn't expect her to understand, he said, "I'm here because I couldn't stay away."

She felt the warmth that radiated from him as he moved closer. She closed her eyes and basked in it.

"I didn't realize how much a part of me you had become until you were gone," he told her.

His breath was a whisper that brushed her hair. He still hadn't touched her, but she could almost feel his hand on her cheek. Her heart hammered against her ribs.

"The thought of never seeing you again hurt like hell," he continued. He touched her then because he had no choice. His fingers grazed her cheek as he stroked the hair away from her face. Silk and cream. Just as he'd remembered. "I'm through running, Dana."

It was as simple as that, he realized. All he'd needed was someone to care enough about to make him want to change—to make him want to stop running. Someone to love.

"I love you," he said tenderly.

Dana's breath caught, then rushed from her. She turned and met the raw emotion in his eyes. "Would you repeat that?"

"I love you."

He couldn't have said it better, she thought. For some silly reason, she felt like crying as she reached up to push her fingers through the hair over his ear. Joyful tears, she decided, blinking them back. "I've waited a long time to hear you say it," she murmured.

For the first time since he'd walked into the room, Michael allowed himself to hope. It was there in the blue-green eyes he'd come to cherish. She'd forgiven him.

He circled her waist and drew her to him. "I was a fool to think I could forget about you," he said, his own voice dropping to a husky timber. "You're a part of me, Dana. It's a feeling I get when you walk into the room. I don't have to see you to know you're here."

A teasing smile curved her lovely mouth. "It was probably those clumpy crutches."

Michael laughed. It was a good feeling. But not as good as her soft curves, pressed against him. Her head was tipped back and she was watching him with open passion in her eyes. Her fingers caressed the nape of his neck, then tangled in his hair to gently pull his head down. Her lips parted in an invitation he had no intention of refusing.

Her kiss was tender, yet demanding. As he knew her love would be. He felt like a lost man who'd found his

way home after a lifetime of searching. He kissed he
jaw, her throat, the junction at her shoulder.

He groaned her name, then brought his face up and
met her gaze. "I'm not fool enough to believe I ca
shrug off my past like it never happened," he said
"It'll always be a part of who I am. But I'm ready t
go on with my life now. And I don't want to do i
alone."

She brushed his lips with feathery kisses. "Yo
don't have to," she assured him. "I'll always be her
for you." He'd come to her—completely. There wa
no way she'd let him go again.

"Would you mind putting that in writing?"

She gave a startled laugh. "What?"

"Marry me?"

Dana didn't have to think about her answer. Sh
loved this man. She wanted to spend the rest of her lif
getting to know him. *All* of him.

"Yes, Michael, I'll marry you."

"I'm not an easy man to live with," he warned
"There may be times when you'll feel like screamin
at me."

Dana couldn't imagine anything easier than livin
with him, but kept the thought to herself. Instead sh
shrugged and said, "That's what it's all about, isn't it
We argue, we learn a little more about each other an
then we make up."

He gave her that sexy, crooked smile of his that al
ways did funny things to her equilibrium. "Making u
sounds nice."

"It can be." She slowly ran a finger down the but
tons of his shirt and seduced him with a smile of he

own. "What are you and your hot tub doing tonight?"

Michael's eyes went dark. "You mean the one without any water left in it?"

"That's the one." She unfastened a button and slid her hand inside his shirt to make direct contact with the warmth of his skin. She had the wild urge to undress him on the spot and it thrilled her.

It also reminded her of something.

"Better yet," she said, her voice low and intimate, "let's go dancing."

There was amusement in his smile as he searched her face. "Dancing?"

"You know what I mean." Her fingers toyed with another button on his shirt. "The one where we have the dance floor to ourselves and our favorite waltz is playing."

Michael pulled her hips closer, letting her know what her teasing was doing to him. "But that was just a fantasy," he whispered.

Dana's smile was pure enchantment. "Not anymore."

* * * * *

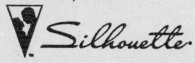

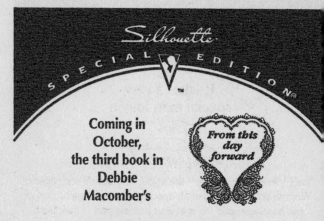

Silhouette

SPECIAL EDITION ™®

Coming in October, the third book in Debbie Macomber's

From this day forward

MARRIAGE WANTED

Dash Davenport didn't marry Savannah Charles for love, only convenience. As a divorce attorney, he knew marriage was a mistake. But as a man, Dash couldn't resist Savannah's charms. It seemed Savannah knew all the makings of a happily-ever-after. And it wasn't long after saying "I do" that Dash started thinking about forever....

FROM THIS DAY FORWARD—Three couples marry first and find love later in this heartwarming trilogy.

Only from Silhouette Special Edition.

Silhouette Books has done it again!

Opening night in October has never been as exciting! Come watch as
the curtain rises and romance flourishes when the stars of tomorrow
make their debuts today!

Revel in Jodi O'Donnell's STILL SWEET ON HIM—
Silhouette Romance #969
...as Callie Farrell's renovation of the family homestead leads her
straight into the arms of teenage crush Drew Barnett!

Tingle with Carol Devine's BEAUTY AND THE BEASTMASTER—
Silhouette Desire #816
...as legal eagle Amanda Tarkington is carried off by wrestler
Bram Masterson!

Thrill to Elyn Day's A BED OF ROSES—
Silhouette Special Edition #846
...as Dana Whitaker's body and soul are healed by sexy physical
therapist Michael Gordon!

Believe when Kylie Brant's McLAIN'S LAW —
Silhouette Intimate Moments #528
...takes you into detective Connor McLain's life as he falls for
psychic—and suspect—Michele Easton!

Catch the classics of tomorrow—*premiering* today—
only from ❦ *Silhouette*

And now for something completely different from Silhouette....

SPELLBOUND
ROMANCE

Every once in a while, Silhouette brings you a book that is truly unique and innovative, taking you into the world of paranormal happenings. And now these stories will carry our special "Spellbound" flash, letting you know that you're in for a truly exciting reading experience!

In October, look for *McLain's Law* (IM #528) by Kylie Brant

Lieutenant Detective Connor McLain believes only in what he can see—until Michele Easton's haunting visions help him solve a case...and her love opens his heart!

McLain's Law is also the Intimate Moments "Premiere" title, introducing you to a debut author, sure to be the star of tomorrow!

Available in October...only from Silhouette Intimate Moments

INTIMATE MOMENTS®
Silhouette®

SPELL1

TAKE A WALK ON THE
DARK SIDE OF LOVE WITH

October is the shivery season, when chill winds blow and
shadows walk the night. Come along with us into a haunting
world where love and danger go hand in hand, where
passions will thrill you and dangers will chill you. Silhouette's
second annual collection from the dark side of love brings
you three perfectly haunting tales from three of our most
bewitching authors:

Kathleen Korbel
Carla Cassidy
Lori Herter

Haunting a store near you this October.

Only from 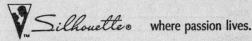 where passion lives.

SHAD93

SILHOUETTE.... Where Passion Lives

Don't miss these Silhouette favorites by some of our most popular authors!
And now, you can receive a discount by ordering two or more titles!

Silhouette Desire®

#05751	THE MAN WITH THE MIDNIGHT EYES BJ James	$2.89
#05763	THE COWBOY Cait London	$2.89
#05774	TENNESSEE WALTZ Jackie Merritt	$2.89
#05779	THE RANCHER AND THE RUNAWAY BRIDE Joan Johnston	$2.89

Silhouette Intimate Moments®

#07417	WOLF AND THE ANGEL Kathleen Creighton	$3.29
#07480	DIAMOND WILLOW Kathleen Eagle	$3.39
#07486	MEMORIES OF LAURA Marilyn Pappano	$3.39
#07493	QUINN EISLEY'S WAR Patricia Gardner Evans	$3.39

Silhouette Shadows®

#27003	STRANGER IN THE MIST Lee Karr	$3.50
#27007	FLASHBACK Terri Herrington	$3.50
#27009	BREAK THE NIGHT Anne Stuart	$3.50
#27012	DARK ENCHANTMENT Jane Toombs	$3.50

Silhouette Special Edition®

#09754	THERE AND NOW Linda Lael Miller	$3.39
#09770	FATHER: UNKNOWN Andrea Edwards	$3.39
#09791	THE CAT THAT LIVED ON PARK AVENUE Tracy Sinclair	$3.39
#09811	HE'S THE RICH BOY Lisa Jackson	$3.39

Silhouette Romance®

#08893	LETTERS FROM HOME Toni Collins	$2.69
#08915	NEW YEAR'S BABY Stella Bagwell	$2.69
#08927	THE PURSUIT OF HAPPINESS Anne Peters	$2.69
#08952	INSTANT FATHER Lucy Gordon	$2.75

	AMOUNT	$ _____
DEDUCT:	10% DISCOUNT FOR 2+ BOOKS	$ _____
	POSTAGE & HANDLING	$ _____
	($1.00 for one book, 50¢ for each additional)	
	APPLICABLE TAXES*	$ _____
	TOTAL PAYABLE	$ _____
	(check or money order—please do not send cash)	

To order, complete this form and send it, along with a check or money order for the
total above, payable to Silhouette Books, to: *In the U.S.*: 3010 Walden Avenue,
P.O. Box 9077, Buffalo, NY 14269-9077; *In Canada*: P.O. Box 636, Fort Erie, Ontario,
L2A 5X3.

Name: _____

Address:_____ City:_____

State/Prov.: _____ Zip/Postal Code:_____

*New York residents remit applicable sales taxes.
Canadian residents remit applicable GST and provincial taxes.

SBACK-O

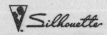